TUTOR IN THE SHADOWS

WHEN PROTECTION BECOMES A PRISON

By Asher W. Lockwell

First published in 2025 by MK Storyworks.

Copyright 2025 by **Asher W. Lockwell**

This book is a work of fiction. Names, characters, businesses, organizations, places, events, and incidents are either the product of the author's imagination or are used fictitiously. Any resemblance to actual persons, living or dead, events, or locales is entirely coincidental.

Printed and bound by MK Storyworks.

TABLE OF CONTENTS

Asher W. Lockwell

Praise For Tutor In The Shadows: When Protection Becomes A Prison

"**Asher W. Lockwell** is the master of the domestic nightmare. An oppressive atmosphere, a devastating twist, and characters you can't trust this is psychological suspense at its finest. I read it in one breathless sitting." *The National Thriller Review*

"The most unnerving look at a supposedly perfect family since that other famous housemaid novel. You will think you know the monster, but Lock has something far more chilling in store. Unputdownable." *Bestselling Author*

"A masterful deployment of tension. Lock uses silence and wealth as weapons. Every page is a step further into a calculated trap. This book defines the modern psychological thriller." *Industry Trade Magazine*

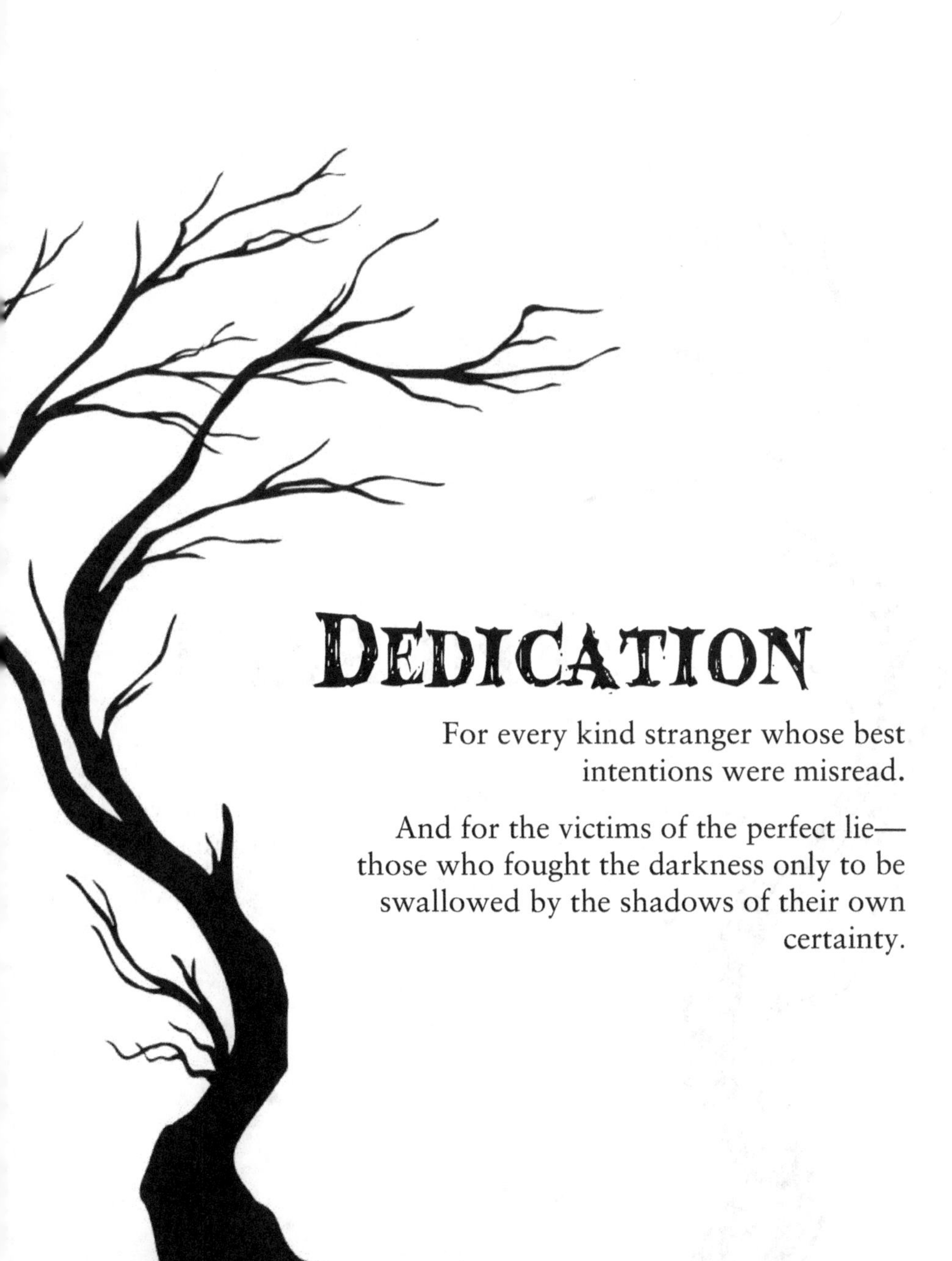

DEDICATION

For every kind stranger whose best
intentions were misread.

And for the victims of the perfect lie—
those who fought the darkness only to be
swallowed by the shadows of their own
certainty.

EPIGRAPH

"The moment you trust, you've
already lost the game."

Anonymous

PART I

THE TRAP

Chapter 1
The Arrival

The gates didn't simply swing open; they retreated heavy and slow groaning on unseen mechanisms like stone teeth yielding to an unwilling patient. Cillian heard the clang a final, definitive sound before the dense treeline parted enough for him to glimpse the estate itself. The sound didn't fade; it cut through the air with metallic finality, sealing the entrance and making the act of passing through feel like a formal sentencing.

The oppressive quiet was the first thing that disturbed him. It was unnatural. Where were the usual sounds of the countryside the distant chatter of birds, the hum of the nearby highway that had followed him for the last thirty miles? There was nothing. It was a complete acoustic vacuum, meticulously designed, Cillian suspected, to strip away every extraneous sound and replace it with the weight of the house itself. It felt less like a natural environment and more like a controlled laboratory where experiments were conducted in isolation.

He drove his beat-up Ford Focus a faded splash of crimson against the severe grey-and-white palette of this manicured world up the impossibly long, gravel-lined drive. The crunching of the tires felt offensively loud. The road wound upward, shielded by ancient, towering oaks that were trimmed too perfectly, creating a tunnel of silent, wealthy judgment.

When the house finally emerged from the mist, it was not merely a house it was a fortress. Sprawling, imposing, and unforgiving, it was built of dark, pitted granite that seemed permanently cold, impervious to the weak autumn sun. It radiated authority, severity, and a chilling indifference to comfort. The architecture was a blend of Neo-Gothic and stark modernism a statement that history and power were both ruthless and eternal.

Cillian's grip tightened on the worn leather of the steering wheel, his one small comfort from the world he'd left behind. He took a deep breath, forcing the tension from his shoulders. His belongings a simple duffel bag filled with sensible sweaters, well-thumbed journals, and notebooks felt hopelessly inadequate, almost vulgar, against this level of granite grandeur. He was a dedicated professional, accustomed to complex, sensitive cases often the sons and daughters of the absurdly wealthy but this was a different league of emotional and physical containment.

He had accepted the job partly for the astonishing salary, recognizing it as a necessary means to fund his own modest ambitions. But more than that, he had taken it for the challenge for the moral imperative. Senator Alistair Ashworth's son, Rhys, was not just wealthy; he was, according to the careful phrasing of the assessments, intensely "delicate" and acutely "withdrawn." Cillian, an empath by nature, felt an instinctive pull toward that kind of vulnerability. It was a sign, he told himself as he checked his composed, professional reflection in the rearview mirror, that he was exactly the right person to save this boy from his overwhelming circumstances.

He parked his small crimson car discreetly beneath the portico, and the front door opened before he could switch off the engine.

The house manager, Mr. Finch, stood waiting. Finch was a perfectly tailored suit over a blank, expressionless face. His movements were economical and devoid of warmth. "Mr. Rains?" he said. His tone made it clear this was not a question but a statement of identification. Without waiting for a reply, he motioned Cillian inside, treating him with the cool efficiency one might show a delivery or perhaps a necessary but temporary inconvenience.

As Cillian stepped over the threshold, the air changed again. The vast hall was meticulously cooled, sterile to the point of discomfort. The dominant scent was a mix of polished wood and something metallic and sharp an expensive, chemical cleanliness that seemed designed to ward off the imperfections of human life. It felt like a mausoleum that had been dusted daily.

He was led through cavernous halls where sound died instantly against heavy velvet drapes and polished stone floors. The walls were lined with portraits of stern-faced ancestors whose eyes followed him with cold, inherited judgment. Every painting was muted all blacks, greys, and oppressive browns forming a visual history of silence. Every Persian rug was precisely centered, every antique piece of furniture looked too fragile, too important, to be touched.

The house didn't feel lived in; it felt curated like a museum dedicated to the idea of a perfect, absent family. Cillian realized these halls were not built for comfort or conversation, but for the suppression of spontaneity.

At last, Finch ushered him into a sitting room dominated by a white marble fireplace and floor-to-ceiling windows overlooking miles of manicured, empty lawns.

A woman was waiting.

Anya Ashworth.

She was, Cillian noted with professional astonishment, strikingly beautiful. Thin to the point of sharpness, she was composed with surgical precision from the severe, dark line of her impeccably styled hair to the immaculate cream suit she wore. She stood by the fireplace, one hand resting on the marble mantel, and didn't offer a handshake. Her stillness was perhaps the most unsettling thing about her. She was a study in practiced control.

"Mr. Rains," she said. Her voice was cool, educated, and carried a faint British inflection, devoid of warmth or invitation. "You drove all this way from London? That must have been draining."

Cillian recognized the game immediately. This wasn't politeness; it was an opening move a way to establish his fatigue, his vulnerability, to make him the supplicant.

"The drive was fine, Mrs. Ashworth," Cillian replied, meeting her gaze without flinching. "I'm here and ready to begin work immediately."

"Work," she repeated, tasting the word as if testing something unfamiliar. "Your references speak highly of your... patience. They note that your empathy is overwhelming. Are you certain you understand the rigor we require? My son, Rhys, needs discipline, Mr. Rains. He does not need coddling."

Cillian caught the deliberate challenge. This wasn't an interview; it was a performance of dominance. She was establishing the hierarchy client above employee, authority above empathy.

"I understand structure, Mrs. Ashworth," he said evenly. "But structure only works when it's built on trust. And trust is built on connection, not control."

Her mouth curved into a faint, brittle smile that never touched her eyes. "Such a modern philosophy. You'll find our home operates on older principles, Mr. Rains. Rhys is delicate sensitive. He does not take well to surprises. For efficiency and minimal disruption, you will follow the schedule provided by Mr. Finch without deviation. You will not discuss family matters, especially those involving my husband's political career, and you will restrict your teaching to designated areas."

She paused, letting the weight of her words settle a list of boundaries that sounded more like bars. "You are here to educate. Nothing more."

"Understood," Cillian said with a nod. Yet an uneasy feeling stirred beneath his professional calm. He had encountered cold, demanding parents before, but Anya's detachment felt different less like arrogance and more like armor shielding something unstable.

The meeting ended abruptly. Anya led him up a sweeping staircase past another gallery of silent ancestors. She moved with deliberate, almost mechanical grace a woman accustomed to the world bending around her.

She stopped before a small, well-furnished room tucked beneath the eaves. "This will be your accommodation," she said flatly. "It is separate from the family wing. We value privacy, Mr. Rains particularly ours."

The room was clean and quiet. Too quiet. It felt less like a guest room and more like an expensive, temporary cell a service space hastily converted for respectable isolation. The walls were thick, the carpet dense. The single window was small and high, overlooking the vast, empty grounds.

Cillian went to it immediately. From this height, he could see the lawns and distant trees, but not the road or gates. He was isolated able to observe but not truly connected. It was the perfect setup for an outsider: visually privileged, sonically cut off.

Anya offered one last, detached reminder about the dinner hour, then departed, her footsteps fading down the hall with clinical precision.

Alone, Cillian unpacked his duffel bag, laying out his worn sweaters and notebooks. He placed his old smartphone on the bedside table his fragile link to the outside world. Standing by the window, he watched the sun sink behind the treeline, shadows stretching across the silent lawn.

The whole estate felt like a beautifully maintained tomb. He was a long way from London and from help. He had come here believing he would save a fragile boy.

But as darkness thickened over the immaculate grounds, a cold dread settled deep in his chest. He began to wonder, with sick certainty, whether he had simply driven too far and stepped willingly, with all his trusting empathy, into a cage.

Chapter 2
The Son

The air in the library was thick and still, smelling intensely of aged paper, dry rot, and polished leather a scent that spoke not of vibrant knowledge, but of accumulated, dusty wealth. It was a vast, dark room, less a space for quiet study and more a formal, intimidating setting designed to demonstrate gravitas and intellectual lineage. The shelves soared impossibly high, the books untouched and bound in uniform, somber colors a silent monument to learning that no one actually engaged in. It was a room that demanded respect through sheer, suffocating scale. Cillian felt immediately that this was not a place conducive to nurturing a fragile mind; it was designed to enforce silence and smallness.

Anya Ashworth was precisely on time. The grandfather clock in the hall chimed four o'clock with a heavy, authoritative toll just as she ushered Rhys into the room.

The boy, sixteen years old, was the complete antithesis of his surroundings a flicker of vulnerability against the granite severity of the house. He looked significantly younger than his age: pale, slight, and almost translucent, with fine, straight blond hair that seemed to absorb light rather than reflect it. His expensive, tailored clothes hung loosely on his thin frame, suggesting recent, anxious weight loss. Cillian watched his movements carefully. Rhys navigated the opulent room with a subtle, perpetual flinch shoulders hunched, head lowered as if expecting the heavy furniture or silent portraits to suddenly lurch out and strike him.

"Rhys, this is Mr. Rains. He will be your tutor."

Anya didn't speak to Rhys. Cillian immediately registered the cold precision of her tone: she spoke *about* him, not *to* him, as though she were giving a report at a clinical briefing rather than introducing her son to a teacher. Her voice was pure functionality, stripped of warmth, reducing the boy to an object of instruction.

"You will refer to him as Mr. Rains. You will listen to his instruction. You will not waste his time."

She delivered the rules as though they were final, immutable laws. Cillian noticed that Rhys offered no acknowledgment, no nod just a barely visible tremor beneath his collar.

Rhys kept his head down, fixated on the intricate geometric pattern of the Turkish rug beneath his polished shoes. Cillian waited quietly, his breathing steady, searching for a human moment perhaps a casual smile, a gentle word, or even a simple handshake something that might break through the boy's obvious terror.

Anya gave him no such chance. She moved directly to the heart of the psychological tension.

"We expect progress in mathematics, Mr. Rains. Specifically, in advanced calculus. Rhys has struggled in the past. His previous tutors, shall we say, utterly failed to connect with his particular sensitivities."

She emphasized the word *sensitivities* with a dry, surgical malice that Cillian recognized instantly it was passive aggression wielded like a scalpel, framing the boy's struggle as a moral failing rather than a difficulty. The message was clear: *He is defective, and if you fail, the defect is yours.*

"I understand," Cillian replied, keeping his voice gentle, deliberately contrasting her clipped tone. His gaze remained fixed on Rhys's lowered head. "We'll start with the foundations, Mrs. Ashworth. We won't worry about calculus yet. We'll take the time needed to build trust."

It was a subtle act of professional defiance one he knew Anya would recognize.

Her sharp eyes narrowed slightly, acknowledging his quiet resistance. After a beat, she tilted her chin. "Trust is a luxury, Mr. Rains. Obedience is a necessity in this house. Now, I have affairs of far greater importance to attend to. Rhys will remain here with you until six o'clock precisely."

With a final, dismissive glance at her son, Anya turned on her heel. The sound of her expensive heels clicking down the hall was the only noise in the oppressive quiet.

As soon as she was gone, Cillian felt the tension in the room shift. The air lightened, though only slightly. Rhys remained rigid, still staring at the rug, but the silence now carried something different less of control, more of vulnerability.

Cillian took a slow breath. He moved his large armchair from its ceremonial place near the fireplace and positioned it across from Rhys at the massive oak desk. He sat with an open posture, careful to seem calm and approachable. He let the silence linger for another moment, refusing to break it with academic demands.

"Hi, Rhys," he said softly. "I know your mother prefers formality, but you can call me Cillian if you'd like. We can keep that between us. It's just us here now."

Rhys didn't answer right away. The silence stretched, amplifying Cillian's own nervousness. Slowly, painfully, the boy lifted his head. When his eyes finally met Cillian's, the effect was startling. They were a pale, piercing blue filled with an intense, quiet fear. It was the gaze of a trapped animal, assessing danger with instinctual dread.

"Mr. Finch said I have to call you Mr. Rains," Rhys whispered, his voice fragile and barely audible.

"We're here to learn, Rhys," Cillian said with a reassuring smile. "And learning shouldn't be ruled by fear or arbitrary rules. We need to make this our space somewhere you feel safe. So tell me, what do you like to read? Not for school, just for yourself."

Rhys flinched. His eyes darted toward the heavy oak door where his mother had vanished, as though expecting her to reappear. His hands were clasped so tightly in his lap that his knuckles were white. This wasn't mere shyness it was the visible residue of long-term fear.

"I like... history," he managed, forcing the words through a constricted throat.

"That's great," Cillian said warmly. "This house, in all its intimidating glory, seems full of history. Maybe we can start there instead of equations today." He paused, letting the quiet stretch in a non-threatening way. "Look, Rhys. I'm not here to judge or pressure you. I can tell this place is heavy. I'm not them. Whatever's happening you don't have to face it alone."

It was a risky move, stepping into forbidden territory, but Cillian couldn't help it. His empathy wasn't calculated it was instinctive. The boy's pain was too visible, too raw.

Rhys's chin trembled, his composure fracturing. "She says… she says if I don't apply myself, if I'm not perfect…" He drew a sharp, shaking breath. "…I'll end up like the last one."

The words fell like shards of glass between them. *The last one.*

"The last one?" Cillian asked gently, already running through possibilities dismissal, breakdown, something worse.

Rhys shook his head violently, panic overtaking him. He clamped his lips shut, his expression closing off completely. Whatever that phrase meant, it was something he could not safely explain.

Cillian didn't push. The truth was clear enough: Anya Ashworth had turned the fate of a previous tutor into a threat a weapon to keep her son in submission.

He leaned forward slightly, keeping his movements slow and deliberate. He placed his hand, palm up, on the desk near Rhys's clenched ones, careful not to touch.

"Rhys," he said quietly, "we'll go at your pace. We'll find your strength. We'll work only when you feel safe. This is your time now not theirs."

Rhys lifted his head again, eyes meeting Cillian's with a quiet, startling depth. For a moment, the fear receded, replaced by something ancient and cautious an understanding beyond his years.

Then he gave a small, almost imperceptible nod.

It was the smallest of gestures, but to Cillian, it felt monumental a fragile bond formed in the wreckage of fear. Relief and resolve flooded through him. The first connection had been made.

Cillian understood then: he had gained the boy's trust, and in doing so, he had accepted the unspoken challenge.

The game had begun. Cillian, the empath and the savior, was now fully enlisted.

Chapter 3
The First Mark

Cillian moved with deliberate, professional caution, choosing to ease Rhys into the academic work. He understood the fundamental psychology of the situation: any direct or sudden pressure from him would only reinforce Rhys's existing trauma, strengthening the boy's reliance on Anya's rigid expectations of compliance rather than Cillian's methods of genuine learning. He needed to be the opposite of the house soft, unstructured, and safe.

The third day of tutoring found them in a different designated room, a sparse, functional study tucked away off the main library wing. The room was dominated by a heavy oak desk and severe, utilitarian shelving. The prevailing quiet of the estate that unnatural acoustic void was interrupted only by the distant, faint, yet incredibly regular ticking of an old grandfather clock somewhere down the long corridor. It was a relentless metronome marking the slow, agonizing passage of time within the cage.

To engage Rhys's mind without triggering his math anxiety, Cillian had shifted to visual activities. He had set Rhys the task of sketching the complex, multifaceted shapes of a dodecahedron, encouraging him to focus on spatial relationships and hidden geometries rather than the cold logic of equations.

"Just try to see the hidden lines, Rhys. It's a puzzle, an exploration of space not a test," Cillian encouraged, his voice low and patient. "You need to find the structure that holds the complexity together."

Rhys sat opposite him, dutifully attempting the sketch. Cillian noted the furrow in his brow, the delicate, unnatural concentration he applied to such a simple task. The boy was meticulous, terrified of making a mistake. He wore an old, thick, oversized sweater a habit Cillian had observed since his arrival. The sweater looked expensive, yet it seemed designed to swallow Rhys's thin frame, his slight body almost disappearing within the heavy wool. The material was slightly bunched up around his elbow.

Then, in an instant of devastating clarity, it happened.

Rhys leaned forward slightly to reach his eraser, intending to correct an infinitesimal error in one of the geometric planes. As he shifted his weight, the cuff of the thick, heavy sweater usually pulled down to his wrist rode up his arm, retracting slightly and bunching near his shoulder.

Cillian saw it instantly. He didn't have time to process the sight; the image simply imprinted itself, fully formed and horrifically clear, onto his mind.

It was a small, distinct bruise. A patch of ugly, mottled purple and yellow discoloration, sitting starkly against the boy's pale, almost translucent skin. The shape was not accidental. It was circular a perfectly defined ring of trauma, the unmistakable, precise mark left by the forceful grip of five adult fingers and a thumb. Cillian's professional mind, trained to observe and interpret, recognized the pattern immediately. It spoke of immense pressure, inflicted by a hand that had not intended to be gentle.

The colors confirmed its age: fading yellow at the perimeter, deep, saturated purple at the center. It was the mark of an injury a few days old recent, but not fresh. The healing cycle was visible, a physical clock counting down the time since the abuse had occurred.

Cillian froze. His internal monologue that constant, low-level stream of professional analysis and assessment went completely silent. The quiet that enveloped him was more profound than any the house had ever offered. He hadn't just suspected abuse based on psychological signs or cold behavior; now he had concrete, physical proof. The bruise was the undeniable crack in the Ashworths' façade the physical manifestation of the psychological cruelty he had sensed.

Rhys, instinctively aware of the sudden, intense cessation of Cillian's energy, noticed the tutor's unblinking, horrified stare.

The boy's reaction was immediate, total, and terrifyingly revealing. He went utterly rigid. His free hand snapped down with lightning speed to yank the heavy cuff of the sweater back over the strip of exposed skin, concealing the injury as if extinguishing a small, dangerous flame. His head bowed instantly, his chin pressed to his chest. His entire body language the sudden contraction, the rigid suppression of movement communicated one word with haunting clarity: shame.

"Rhys?" Cillian asked, his voice catching slightly as he forced himself to keep the pitch neutral and low, careful not to startle the panicked boy. The slightest tremor of anger or shock, he knew, would send him retreating completely.

"I... I made a mess of the drawing," Rhys whispered, his breath catching in his throat, uneven and desperate. "The geometry is too hard. Can we stop now, Cillian? Please?"

The use of Cillian's first name, offered in such a moment of raw, desperate pleading, was all the confirmation he needed. Rhys wasn't ashamed of the drawing, which was perfectly adequate; he was terrified of being discovered terrified that Cillian had seen and now knew the truth.

"Yes, of course," Cillian said quickly, moving to cover the exposed emotional ground and deliberately dismissing the drawing with an air of calm reassurance. He gathered the pencils and tidied the sheets of paper, giving Rhys a clear, nonverbal signal of protection and alliance. "We're done for today, Rhys. Don't worry about the drawing. Get some rest."

It was a promise of safety a silent vow that Cillian would keep his secret.

But the sanctuary was short-lived.

Just as Cillian was ushering Rhys toward the study door planning to deliver him safely back to the anonymity of the main house it happened. The unmistakable sound of Anya Ashworth's light, quick heels clicked on the marble floor of the corridor, growing louder, closer, and more demanding with every step.

Anya entered the study without knocking. Her entrance was an invasion, her presence immediately flooding the small room with cold, sharp authority. Her eyes swept the space instantly a high-speed, three-point inspection: the scattered pencils, the incomplete geometry sketch, Rhys's small, distraught face, and Cillian's overly concerned, protective posture.

She didn't ask what was wrong. She didn't need to. She simply looked at Rhys with a piercing, cold stare an expression Cillian instantly recognized as controlled fury, the barely contained, white-hot rage of a woman whose meticulous performance had been momentarily disrupted.

"Rhys, I trust you haven't been overly dramatic for Mr. Rains?" she asked, her tone cutting and casual, the implication of the word *dramatic* a deliberate dismissal of his genuine distress.

Rhys flinched again, retreating a subtle step further behind Cillian, leaning into the tutor's protective space without thinking.

"Rhys simply needs time to adjust, Mrs. Ashworth. We've finished for the day," Cillian interjected smoothly, immediately positioning himself between Anya and her son a physical act of defiance he hoped she would recognize as a clear boundary.

Anya's lips thinned into a sharp, pale line. She held Cillian's gaze, her eyes cold and judgmental. "Adjustment is only necessary when one has been allowed to deviate, Mr. Rains. Please remember that. This is not a summer camp. And Rhys, if you continue to be so unreliable, I will have to find other means of managing your sensitivities."

The veiled threat the sinister suggestion of "other means" was delivered with chilling clarity, a further confirmation of the psychological warfare Cillian had suspected. She dismissed him with a cool nod, a final assertion of control, before marching Rhys away toward the main wing of the house.

Cillian stood alone, his hands still clutching the pencils. The sheer audacity of the woman to issue an explicit, veiled threat immediately after he had seen the physical evidence sent a spike of pure, burning righteousness through him.

He waited for ten long minutes, listening to the silence resettle around him a stillness now heavy with conspiracy.

Later, back in the oppressive quiet of his attic room, Cillian pulled out his phone. He couldn't shake the image of the purple-and-yellow mark. For the next hour, he meticulously researched forensic information: accidental injuries, the timeline of blood clotting, the specific patterns of forced gripping. He compared images of various trauma types.

He dismissed every possibility of a clumsy fall, a sporting injury, or an accident. The mark was too distinct, too circular, too perfect a negative impression of an adult hand. Rhys's reaction the instant panic and shame was too authentic to be faked.

It was not a fall. It was not a game. It was a statement.

Cillian felt the immense weight of the truth. This was no longer suspicion; it was confirmation. This was physical evidence a moral imperative that transcended his paid employment. He had come here as a tutor. He would leave as a protector.

He had to save this boy before the situation escalated further. The cold, sterile reality of the Ashworth Estate was an immaculate mask, and Cillian had finally, fleetingly, glimpsed the ugly, rotten thing it was hiding.

He stood by the window, staring out at the isolating expanse of the manicured lawn. The immense, impossible task lay before him. He was Rhys's only chance, and his protective instinct his overwhelming empathy, the very trait Anya had warned against had now become his only weapon.

He had to move beyond tutoring. He had to start investigating.

<h1 style="text-align:center">CHAPTER 4</h1>
<h1 style="text-align:center">THE UNSEEN CAMERA</h1>

The shock that had seized Cillian upon seeing the purple-and-yellow bruise had given way not to measured contemplation, but to a frantic, overwhelming sense of urgency. The physical evidence was now a burning reality an unignorable mandate for action.

Cillian spent the morning pacing his attic room, running through countless mental simulations of what might happen if he simply picked up the phone and called the local constabulary.

The result was always the same: failure.

He imagined the Ashworths' polished, immediate response Anya's cool, aristocratic denial delivered with a practiced lack of emotion. The Senator's lawyers, a circle of ruthless, highly paid protectors of the family reputation, would descend instantly, dismissing Cillian as a "disgruntled, overly empathetic young man" who had "read far too much into a minor domestic incident."

The bruise would be explained away as a "clumsy fall during a private therapy session." And the final, devastating outcome would be the quiet disappearance of Rhys into some private, untraceable facility while the "pending investigation" conveniently stalled. Cillian would be dismissed, sued into professional ruin, and branded unreliable. His truth would be crushed beneath their power.

He needed proof, proof that could survive a smear campaign backed by Alistair Ashworth's wealth and influence. He needed something objective, irrefutable, and digital.

Cillian's thoughts turned immediately to surveillance. He knew the exterior of the estate was heavily monitored: cameras watched the gates, the drive, and the treeline, recording every movement. But inside the mansion, there was an eerie absence of visible cameras. The Ashworths valued their privacy too much to allow lenses to intrude upon their domestic life. Their wealth was its own form of security, relying on isolation and the silence of their staff.

His gaze fell on his old smartphone the one he'd placed on his bedside table upon arrival. It was an older model, a relic he used mainly for emails and the occasional message to Daniel, a former colleague and friend. Still, it had a decent high-resolution camera. Most importantly, Cillian had kept it free from social media and personal apps. It was, for all intents and purposes, a clean slate.

This device, he realized, would not just be his lifeline. It would be his private vault of evidence.

The decision was made, cold and absolute. During the next scheduled lesson, Cillian would act.

The tutoring session took place in a large, rarely used sitting room, draped in velvet and heavy tapestries. Rhys sat quietly beside him, seemingly absorbed in a complex historical timeline Cillian had prepared about European political shifts.

Cillian leaned in slightly, lowering his voice. "Rhys, I'm sorry about yesterday," he began, testing the waters. "Your mother's temper was completely unwarranted. It was cruel."

Rhys looked up at once, his clear blue eyes wide, his fear unmistakable. "You shouldn't say that, Cillian. She hears everything."

"Does she?" Cillian asked softly, leaning closer, his tone conspiratorial. "Even in here? Beyond these heavy drapes?"

Rhys gave a small, defeated shrug, the movement of someone conditioned to silence. "Sometimes I think she has eyes everywhere."

Cillian saw his opening. He placed his hand flat on the table, steady and calm. "I need you to focus on this timeline, Rhys. I've forgotten a textbook in my room the one on the fall of the Roman Empire. I'll just grab it. Keep working, and don't worry about her, alright?"

Rhys nodded quickly, his anxiety channeling into a trembling, obsessive focus on the historical dates.

Cillian didn't go to his attic room. Instead, he slipped out of the sitting room, closing the heavy oak door with agonizing care. He checked the hall empty. The silence was complete. Then he moved swiftly toward the main wing and Rhys's private bedroom, a place he had never been allowed to enter.

To his surprise, the door was unlocked. A chill ran down

his spine. Was it an oversight or an invitation?

He stepped inside and closed the door, listening to the faint click of the latch.

The room was immaculate, almost unnervingly so. There were no posters, no clothes out of place, no trace of teenage chaos no sign of individuality or joy. It was clean, controlled, and stripped of personality. The only personal object was a small, locked wooden box, placed perfectly in the center of the massive oak desk.

Cillian's pulse quickened. He pulled out his phone. He didn't need Rhys for this. What he needed was context the visual evidence of the boy's imprisonment.

He moved carefully, snapping photos: the bare cream-colored walls, the absence of personal items, the locked wooden box. He crouched low, angling the phone to capture a large, locked mahogany cupboard half-hidden behind a decorative screen. Imprisonment. Isolation. Control. The story of psychological abuse was already clear in those images.

He adjusted the angle to focus on the cupboard's keyhole when he heard it a faint, unmistakable sound. The whisper of silk, followed by the soft, deliberate thud of a closing door from the hall below.

Anya.

She was either returning to her office or coming upstairs.

The possibility of discovery froze him.

Cillian reacted on instinct. He dove behind a massive brocaded armchair near the window, pressing himself into its deep folds of velvet. His breath caught violently in his throat. He clutched the phone to his chest, terrified that even the faintest sound the click of a camera shutter would expose him.

His heart thundered against the device, his vision swimming with adrenaline.

The footsteps didn't stop at Rhys's door. They paused he could almost feel her presence, cold and assessing then slowly moved away, fading down the carpeted hall toward the stairs.

Cillian stayed perfectly still for a full minute after the last sound faded, counting the seconds, his mouth dry with fear. When he finally stood, his hands were shaking, sweat dripping down his temples. He looked once more at the locked cupboard the silent symbol of what he'd risked. He had just endangered his job, his freedom, and perhaps Rhys's last hope all for a few shaky photographs.

He shoved the phone into his pocket and hurried back to the sitting room.

Rhys was exactly as he'd left him, eyes fixed on the timeline, motionless and tense.

"Everything alright?" Cillian asked, forcing calm into his voice.

Rhys looked up, eyes troubled. "I heard something. Outside. Near the stairwell."

Cillian swallowed hard. "Probably just Mr. Finch or one of the maids. Don't worry. I found the book let's continue."

Later that evening, in the oppressive quiet of his attic room, Cillian reviewed the photos. They were imperfect and circumstantial, but they were still proof of a sterile environment built not for a child's growth, but for control.

He spent the next hour creating a digital fortress. He hid the photos in an encrypted album, locked behind a complex passcode only he would remember. This phone, he decided, would be his sole vault of evidence. He wrapped it tightly in a sock and hid it deep under his mattress, far from sight.

Cillian leaned back against the wall, his deception weighing heavily on him. It was a violation of trust, a dangerous escalation, and a moral compromise. But innocence, he realized, was a liability here. To fight the Ashworths, he had to become just as cunning as they were.

He didn't care about his guilt. He cared about Rhys.

The phone was his necessary lie his private confession.

And the only thing that might save them both.

The adrenaline from the night of photography the near ·miss, the violent surge of fear while hiding behind the chair had left Cillian physically shaken, but it had also cemented his resolve. The danger felt profoundly real now, validating his decision to gather secret digital proof. He was no longer battling a vague domestic coldness; he was engaged in a surveillance war with Anya Ashworth. He knew she was watching him, tracking his energy and deviations, and he needed a subtle, professionally justifiable way to continue probing the house's physical and psychological boundaries without triggering her suspicion.

He spent a restless, hyper-vigilant night formulating his next move. The direct academic tutoring felt futile, a thin mask over a deeper, life-or-death struggle. He decided to leverage his role by returning to visual and spatial activities, disguising his investigative work under a harmless, educational exercise.

"We're going to work on spatial awareness today, Rhys," Cillian announced as they settled into the study the same room where the bruise had been revealed, its memory still clinging to the air like residual trauma. "Forget geometry, forget the abstract logic. We're going to map the estate. Not for me, but for you. Know your environment."

Cillian spread a large, heavy sheet of blank artist's paper across the desk. He explained the task with calm professionalism: they would draw the house's footprint and the surrounding grounds from memory. It was an exercise in cognitive recall and memory mapping and for Cillian, a systematic cataloging of potential escape routes and hidden zones.

Rhys, ever the dutiful pupil, initially complied. He meticulously sketched the central areas of the house he knew: the library, the dining hall, the main stairwell. His strokes were precise, careful, and almost mechanical an expression of the disciplined anxiety Cillian had come to recognize.

Cillian watched him, waiting for a natural pause. Rhys soon finished the main residential wings, drawing a flawless perimeter. But the sketch revealed a large, unmapped blank space where the structure suddenly became indistinct a wing that jutted out mysteriously on the estate's northern boundary.

"What about the older parts, Rhys?" Cillian asked casually, pointing to the unfinished section. He kept his tone light, almost offhand. "The North Wing, right there. What's in that section? Is it residential? Storage? What does that part of the house contain?"

Rhys's hand, which had been moving with careful rhythm, froze. The charcoal pencil slipped soundlessly from his fingers and landed on the paper. The tension that seized him was instant and complete.

"It's… it's dusty," Rhys mumbled, his voice shrinking as his eyes darted toward the door, then back to the page. He avoided Cillian's gaze. "It's off-limits. Mom says. Always has been."

"Off-limits to everyone?" Cillian asked gently, pressing a little further.

Rhys shivered a subtle but unmistakable confirmation that the area was more than "dusty." It was forbidden, a place of secrecy and consequence.

Cillian felt a quiet surge of triumph. He had found his next lead. But the moment of discovery was brutally interrupted.

Anya entered the room.

It was uncanny. Her timing was always perfect arriving precisely when Cillian veered off-script or when Rhys showed a flicker of vulnerability. It was as if she possessed an internal alarm wired directly to their moments of subversion.

Her eyes went straight to the desk. They narrowed the instant they landed on the sketch specifically, on the blank, unlabeled section Rhys was now trying desperately to conceal with his arm.

"Rhys," she said, her voice sharp as breaking glass. She crossed the room slowly, her disapproval radiating with icy authority. "Mr. Rains is here to teach mathematics and history. Not cartography. Not architecture. That wing is unstable. It's too cold for long periods, and you know you're sensitive to the damp. Focus on your work."

The subtext hit like a physical blow: *I know what you're doing. I see your questions. Stay in your lane, tutor, or you'll regret it.*

She didn't address Cillian directly, but the message couldn't have been clearer.

Anya lingered for an agonizing few minutes, overseeing them with chilling intensity. Only after she watched Cillian tuck the forbidden sketchpad away did she finally leave, her exit punctuated by the cold, final click of the door.

Cillian leaned back, rubbing his temples as the adrenaline ebbed into cold resolve. He looked at Rhys, whose posture remained stiff and alert. "Unstable, huh? Or secret?"

Rhys said nothing. His eyes stayed fixed on the closed door. But then, in a small, nearly imperceptible gesture, he tilted his chin toward a high, forgotten shelf near the ceiling, where a stack of old, discolored art history textbooks gathered dust.

Cillian understood immediately. Rhys wasn't just a frightened boy he was a quiet collaborator, communicating through unspoken signals.

When the lesson ended and Rhys was dismissed for the day, Cillian waited until the house sank into its usual evening silence. Then he went to the shelf. Climbing the wobbling library ladder, his hands trembling slightly, he retrieved the indicated textbook. It was large and heavy, its pages yellowed with age and thick with dust.

Wedged deep within its center was a torn piece of parchment. It wasn't a letter or a drawing just a small scrap of paper with a faint pencil inscription, barely visible against the aged surface.

It read: **"The key is where the dead things bloom."**

A chill ran through Cillian, sharp and electric. This wasn't the frightened plea of a child it was a deliberate message. A code. Rhys wasn't just a victim waiting to be rescued; he was an active conspirator, leaving clues that required interpretation.

Cillian tucked the parchment safely into his shirt pocket, pressing it against his chest. He repeated the words silently: *The key is where the dead things bloom.*

Then everything clicked. He remembered Finch mentioning an old conservatory attached to the North Wing a once-grand structure built to house exotic tropical plants. The heating system had failed decades ago, and the space had been abandoned ever since. The plants had died long ago, leaving behind only skeletal vines and decaying greenery.

The dead things bloom. It was the perfect, haunting code.

The conservatory, remote and soundproof, connected directly to the forbidden wing. Rhys had given him two vital clues: the location of the key the conservatory and the location of the secret the North Wing itself.

Cillian's path was clear. He would investigate the conservatory first. He needed to find the key to the North Wing, and he needed to do it tonight.

The game had shifted from cautious observation to active infiltration. And Cillian, the reluctant spy, knew he was running out of time before Anya's patience or her *other means* ran out completely.

CHAPTER 6
THE GHOST IN THE LIBRARY

The night outside the vast, silent house was thick and suffocating, pressing down on the estate beneath a heavy, starless sky. The moon, though high, was thin and hazy, offering no real light only a faint gray smear against the blackness, utterly incapable of piercing the house's thick defenses.

Cillian moved through the echoing halls of Ashworth Estate, a clumsy, misplaced shadow in a world of professional ghosts. He relied entirely on his phone's weak, pinprick flashlight, set to the lowest beam a futile gesture against the crushing darkness, but necessary to avoid discovery. His mind clung desperately to the memory of the floor plan he had pieced together, guiding him through the maze of wealth and silence.

He was dressed in the few black clothes he owned outfits meant for a night out in the city, not for breaking and entering. He felt both ridiculous and terrified. Every instinct screamed that he was an intruder violating a sacred, wealthy trust. *I am no thief, no spy; I am a tutor,* his conscience repeated, a high-pitched whine of self-doubt. But that hesitation was instantly silenced by the heavy, righteous conviction that Rhys's life was in danger. That belief gave him a reckless kind of courage the courage of a desperate amateur facing a professional enemy.

His target was the conservatory, the chilling location Rhys had cryptically described as the place where the "dead things bloom." It was a perfect, sinister piece of poetic code.

He found the heavy wooden door leading to the glass wing tucked away off the North Wing corridor. It was exactly as he expected secured with a large, antique brass tumbler lock. The key from the ring he'd found was useless; that one was a skeleton key, and this lock required something far more specific. Cillian knelt, the brass cold beneath his gloved fingers, and confirmed the security was too strong for his untrained hands.

Frustrated, he turned toward the nearby library, reasoning that a key for such a specialized area a wing rarely used and only accessed by the house manager or maintenance might be kept somewhere discreet within the estate's intellectual heart.

The library was enormous, swallowing Cillian and his narrow beam of light whole. It smelled of dry rot, stale air, and aged leather a suffocating scent of wealth slowly decaying under its own weight. His flashlight swept across the endless rows of leather-bound volumes, their identical spines reflecting no character, only the cold uniformity of collection.

He began his search, slow and methodical. He checked the obvious places first the red herrings of domestic secrecy: the ornate key bowls on the side tables, the deep, felt-lined drawers of the massive central desk, and the mantelpiece beneath the grand clock. Nothing. He checked under the cushions of the reading chairs, inside antique snuff boxes every place an owner might think was a "clever" hiding spot. The search was futile; the Ashworths were too meticulous for such carelessness.

He was about to give up, convinced Rhys's clue must have referred to a different key, when his beam caught a high, obscure shelf dedicated entirely to ancient Greek and Latin classics. These were books no one least of all a modern wealthy family would ever touch. The shelf felt forgotten, sealed by time.

Cillian dragged a wobbly, antique mahogany step stool across the rug, its legs scraping softly. It was heavy and unsteady. He climbed onto the highest step, the wood groaning beneath him, certain the entire house could hear it.

Reaching the upper shelf, his heart pounded a frantic rhythm in his ears. He checked behind the ancient spines one by one. Behind a particularly large copy of *The Odyssey*, his fingers brushed something unexpected. It wasn't the brittle texture of paper or cloth it was cold, hard leather.

He carefully eased the heavy book aside and drew the object out with agonizing slowness, afraid of the smallest sound. It was a journal not a simple notebook, but a thick, imposing volume bound in dark leather with aged pages and a heavy silver clasp. The metal caught his flashlight's reflection, gleaming cold and sharp. The journal was too ornate, too carefully hidden to belong to Rhys, the supposed owner of the locked wooden box in his room.

Cillian felt a dizzying certainty: this had to be Anya Ashworth's private diary. If the bruise was proof of her violence, and the conservatory the lock on her secrets, then this was her written confession the truth of her cruelty in her own words.

His heart began to race again, beating hard against his ribs. He clutched the journal to his chest, the hard leather pressing into him, ready to climb down and flee to safety.

That was the precise moment the house decided to awaken.

It wasn't the sharp click of Anya's heels but a soft, distant thump from the floor below, followed by the faint, unmistakable sound of the house manager, Mr. Finch, clearing his throat.

Someone was awake. Someone was moving. Someone was patrolling.

Cillian instantly killed his light, plunging the vast library into suffocating darkness. His mind screamed at him to run, adrenaline surging through his body.

He climbed down blindly from the stool, gripping the journal tightly beneath his sweater. He made a desperate dash for the library door, guided only by instinct and the ghost of memory. Just as he reached it, a thin beam of light Finch's flashlight flickered beneath the gap of the hallway door, only twenty feet away.

Cillian froze, pressing his body flat against the cold wall, hardly daring to breathe. His muscles locked with tension, his heartbeat roaring in his ears. He imagined Finch's cautious eyes scanning the hall, his footsteps soundless on the carpet.

The light passed. The footsteps paused, then slowly retreated toward the kitchen wing. Finch, Cillian concluded, was either making a late-night patrol of the lower floors or simply getting a drink before bed.

It had been too close humiliatingly, terrifyingly close.

Cillian waited five minutes an eternity measured by the hammering of his heart before daring to move again. He crept back to his attic room, every floorboard groaning beneath his weight. Sweat beaded his forehead, and his hands trembled. The journal no longer felt like evidence it felt like a burden, one that could destroy him if discovered.

Once the door to his small room was locked and silence returned, Cillian set the journal on his desk. He ran his thumb over the intricate silver clasp. It was beautiful, ornate, and impossibly secure.

He had finally found the ultimate evidence Anya Ashworth's deepest secret. But the truth was locked tight, sealed by centuries of craftsmanship. He had risked everything for a powerful secret he still had no idea how to open.

CHAPTER 7
THE UNSETTLING GIFT

The locked journal sat on Cillian's bedside table a constant, irritating presence. He tried every careful method he knew prying with a paperclip, tapping the clasp but the lock was well made. Forcing it would only damage the leather and destroy the evidence inside.

He waited for another clue from Rhys, but the boy was silent the next morning. Rhys seemed withdrawn again, avoiding Cillian's gaze as if regretting his boldness from the previous night. Cillian wondered whether Rhys had been punished, or if his nerves had simply worn thin.

The lesson that morning was tense. Rhys struggled through a simple geometry problem, sighing heavily.

"Rhys," Cillian said, setting his pen down. "It's fine. We'll come back to it."

Rhys looked up, his expression shifting suddenly from distress to an unnerving focus. He pushed a small object across the desk.

It was a tiny, rectangular trinket box, crudely made from a soft, lightweight wood. One corner was chipped clearly the work of an amateur.

"What's this?" Cillian asked.

"I made it in shop class," Rhys said quietly. "A long time ago. They were going to throw it out."

Cillian knew Rhys's schedule didn't include shop class, but he didn't challenge him. Rhys was offering him a gift a gesture of trust and alliance.

"It's beautiful, Rhys," Cillian said, picking up the box. It was feather-light.

"It has a good hinge," Rhys continued, watching him closely. "You should use it to keep... important things. Mom hates messy people. She throws away everything she doesn't like."

The last sentence carried a subtle emphasis a warning. *Anya throws things away.*

Rhys was giving Cillian a hiding place. Cillian immediately understood the real message. Rhys was helping him conceal the journal. The box was small, but just large enough to hold Cillian's phone, his evidence vault and, with some care, the leather-bound journal.

"I will," Cillian promised, meeting Rhys's eyes. A wave of gratitude rose within him. Rhys was fighting back in the only ways he could.

Cillian spent the rest of the day carefully concealing his key items. He wrapped the journal in a piece of felt and placed it inside the box along with the phone. Then he hid the box deep in the bottom drawer of his chest, beneath a stack of thick winter sweaters. It was far safer than the vulnerable spot beneath his mattress.

When he finished, Cillian realized how far he had gone. He wasn't just Rhys's tutor anymore. He was his confidant his co-conspirator drawn into a quiet war against the Ashworths.

That night, despite the constant unease, Cillian felt a renewed sense of purpose. He had Rhys's trust, and he had Anya's secret secured. Now he only needed one final piece the key that would unlock the entire terrifying truth.

CHAPTER 8

THE SHADOW IN THE HALL

The discovery of the journal and the frantic hiding of the evidence box had pushed Cillian from concerned employee to full-blown paranoia. He started measuring his steps, timing his movements, and constantly checking over his shoulder.

Anya Ashworth, meanwhile, had subtly increased her surveillance. She began appearing without warning. She wouldn't enter the tutoring room, but Cillian would catch a glimpse of her shadow pausing just outside the door. He'd hear the faint, soft click of the doorknob turning, only for the door to remain closed evidence that she was testing whether they were locked inside or if Cillian was trying to keep her out.

His sleep became fragmented. Every creak in the sprawling old house was a footstep; every gust of wind against his attic window was a whisper. He found himself constantly checking the small, crude trinket box hidden beneath the sweaters.

During a rare, brief conversation with Mr. Finch, the house manager, Cillian made a critical slip. He had been asking about the house's security features, trying to find out whether there were any hidden cameras in the attic hallway.

"The place is massive," Cillian said, attempting to sound casual. "Must be hard to keep everything secure. I haven't seen any cameras inside, which seems a bit risky for a family of this prominence."

Mr. Finch paused, his expression perfectly blank. "The family prefers privacy over security, Mr. Rains. We rely on discretion, not technology." Then he gave Cillian a long, deliberate look that felt less like an answer and more like a warning.

Cillian immediately regretted bringing it up. He was looking for cameras; they were looking for suspicion.

The next day, an email appeared in Cillian's general inbox an impersonal, formal message from the Senator's private account.

Subject: *Professional Boundaries*

Mr. Rains,

I have been apprised of your dedication to Rhys's education. While enthusiasm is appreciated, please remember that the terms of your employment focus strictly on academic instruction. We value professional boundaries and expect them to be upheld rigorously. Should this continue to be an issue, we will be forced to reconsider the terms of your placement.

Senator Alistair Ashworth

The email was cold, efficient, and deeply unsettling. Anya hadn't just been watching she had reported him to her powerful husband, and now Cillian's job was at risk. They knew he was digging.

The house no longer felt like an isolated estate; it felt like enemy territory. Cillian was the intruder, and the inhabitants were closing in. He felt the suffocating presence of the house tightening around him.

They know, he thought, gripping the edge of his desk until his knuckles went white. *They know I'm looking, and they want me gone.*

His escape had to happen soon before he was officially dismissed, and before Rhys was lost forever.

CHAPTER 9
THE KEY TO THE PAST

The Senator's email had given Cillian a terrifying deadline. He could not risk dismissal; the moment he was gone, Rhys would be at Anya's mercy. He had to open the journal. Now.

Cillian spent hours staring at the silver clasp. He researched the clasp on his laptop and tried generic lockpicking tutorials, which predictably failed. He decided he needed professional help, but he could not possibly bring the journal to a town locksmith.

He focused instead on the key itself. The clasp was ornate and antique. He searched online for "antique journal clasps" and "Victorian silver lockets," eventually finding an obscure forum post referencing the style. The post mentioned a specific, old-school locksmith operating out of a tiny village thirty miles away who specialized in repairing such mechanisms.

Cillian fabricated an emergency excuse: he needed specialized textbooks for Rhys's advanced curriculum that could only be found in a particular bookshop in the distant town of Marston. Anya granted the request with a cool, suspicious nod.

The drive was frantic. Cillian felt like a prisoner on temporary parole. He bypassed the bookshop and found the locksmith's dusty, Dickensian shop tucked down a narrow lane.

The old man behind the counter, Silas, wore thick glasses and smelled of oil and metal. Cillian, sweating and nervous, pulled out a photo of the journal clasp he had taken during his research, making sure no background was visible.

"I have a family heirloom," Cillian explained, trying to sound casual. "A journal. The key is lost. I need a replacement key cut from the clasp itself."

Silas adjusted his glasses and looked at the photo with a practiced eye. "Ah, the S-clasp. Pre-war European. Beautiful work. Very secure. I can't cut a key from a photo, son. I need the clasp itself. And I won't damage it, mind you."

Cillian hesitated. He could not bring the evidence here. "What about the key?" he persisted. "Is it a unique cut?"

Silas smiled with a dry, knowing look. "Unique, yes, but not complicated. These types of locks were often sold with a universal master key blank that could open similar mechanisms, though the specific notches would vary. The key itself is usually hidden somewhere obvious. On a large, old ring, perhaps? Check the places they think are clever behind books or in a dried flower vase."

He handed Cillian a plain, uncut silver key blank that looked exactly like what Cillian imagined the real key should look like. "If you find the right ring, the key will be on it. Look for keys that don't belong to a door. Keys to a memory, boy. A secret."

Cillian paid him, thanked him profusely, and drove back with his mind racing. Keys to a memory. Keys that do not belong to a door. Silas had confirmed his suspicion: the key was somewhere on the estate, hidden in plain sight.

He just had to find the right antique ring.

He returned to the house, exhausted but newly energized. He had a mission. He would find the ring, open the journal, and secure the truth before Anya could get rid of him.

Chapter 10
The Hidden Ring

Cillian's paranoia was now laser-focused. He spent his free hours searching the main, common rooms of the house, looking for anything that resembled a hidden key ring. He avoided the tutoring sessions and his bedroom areas he knew Rhys might be watching and concentrated on Anya's territory: the drawing rooms, the formal dining hall, and the sitting room where he had first been interviewed.

The search was meticulous but yielded nothing but dust and expensive porcelain.

Then he remembered Silas's words: *"Check the places they think are clever behind books, or in a dried flower vase."*

He entered Anya's formal, rarely used sitting room. It was decorated in muted greens and creams, cold and lifeless. In the corner stood a large, ornate china cabinet filled with antique vases and figurines. It felt like the kind of place a key would be hidden, relying on its own obviousness.

Cillian approached the cabinet. His eyes scanned the items until they landed on a squat, dark blue ceramic bowl. It didn't look particularly valuable, and it held a few antique linen napkins.

He reached inside the bowl. Beneath the linen, his fingers brushed against cold metal.

He pulled out a heavy, ornate key ring. It held four keys: one large, gothic iron key that looked medieval; two smaller, modern keys; and a final, thin silver key that was antique and perfectly matched the style of the blank Silas had shown him.

Cillian's heart hammered. He had found it the key to the North Wing and, more importantly, the key to Anya's most private thoughts.

He slid the thin silver key off the ring and tucked it into his pocket, replacing the ring exactly where he had found it. The whole process took less than thirty seconds.

He retreated to his room, his victory a silent scream trapped in his chest.

Once behind the locked door, Cillian pulled the thin key from his pocket. He retrieved Anya's journal from the trinket box and placed it on his desk. The moment had arrived.

He inserted the key into the silver clasp. There was a satisfying metallic click, and the clasp sprang open.

Cillian stared at the unlocked journal, his hand trembling. He didn't open the cover immediately. He just stared at the heavy, leather-bound volume the physical embodiment of the cruelty he knew was happening downstairs.

He was no longer speculating. He was about to read the psychological confession of a monster. This key, this journal, was the proof he needed to bring the Ashworth house of cards crashing down.

He took a deep breath, banished all fear, and pulled back the cover.

The truth waited, silent and terrifying, on the pages within.

CHAPTER 11

THE PRIVATE CONFESSION

The journal was not a handwritten diary. It was a collection of printed pages, interrupted by frantic, handwritten notes in Anya's angular script. It read more like a manifesto or a strategy document than a personal diary.

Cillian skimmed the first few pages and found notes about donor lists, political appearances, and party guest lists. He almost dismissed it as a business journal, but then the tone changed.

He stopped abruptly, his eyes fixed on a printed page that laid out specific, rigid rules. A handwritten note was scrawled across the margin.

"I cannot show weakness. He knows my flaws. I must contain him for the stability of the family. If he breaks, everything we built fails."

Cillian felt a cold sweat break out on his forehead. He realized: it had to be Rhys. Contain him.

He flipped forward, searching for similar sections. He found another printed page detailing psychological strategies for dominance, with Anya's angry scribbles in the margin.

"This pathetic defiance must end. I need total silence. He needs to learn obedience; it is for his own good. His emotional outbursts are unacceptable. I will not let him undermine my reputation."

The confirmation hit Cillian like a physical blow. There was no ambiguity. Anya was not writing about her husband or her political career; she was describing the systematic, cruel control of her son. The words matched the bruises, the isolation, and the constant fear Rhys showed. She was documenting her own cruelty.

Cillian scrambled for his phone. He switched on the camera flash and began taking rapid, high-resolution photographs of the most incriminating pages. The harsh light revealed the elegant handwriting and the damning words: contain, dominance, obedience, unacceptable.

This was not circumstantial. This was the motive and the means. He had the confession.

He paused, heart racing, and looked at the phone screen. He had photos of the bruise, and now he had photos of the psychological torture manifesto.

He tried to reconcile the elegant, poised woman downstairs with the chilling voice in the journal. But it made perfect sense.

Anya was a control freak. Rhys was the one thing she could not control, and she was breaking him down methodically.

Cillian carefully locked the journal and replaced it in Rhys's gift box. He then deleted the photos from the main camera roll and secured copies in the hidden evidence vault.

He had everything he needed. But reading those words, especially "contain him," told him he could not wait for a lawyer or a police report. He had to get Rhys out now. The rescue mission was officially greenlit.

CHAPTER 12
THE SENATOR'S ABSENCE

The discovery of the journal and the evidence it contained strengthened Cillian's resolve to escape. But the house was about to become even more dangerous.

The next morning, Senator Alistair Ashworth left for a crucial, multi-day political conference overseas. Cillian learned this not from the family, but from a hushed conversation between the house manager and a groundskeeper. The senator's departure removed the only figure of external authority, leaving Anya in complete, unchallenged control.

Cillian noticed Rhys's quiet, tense stillness throughout the morning. Rhys seemed to understand that the balance had shifted that Anya's dominance was now absolute.

Anya appeared in the library, radiating a cold authority Cillian hadn't seen before. She was sharp, decisive, and entirely focused on him.

"Mr. Rains," she said not asked. "The library is proving disruptive. The house manager informs me that the North Wing Conservatory is rarely used and is soundproof. Effective immediately, you will conduct all future tutoring sessions there. You will use the service entrance for access."

Cillian knew the place. The abandoned glass structure the one from Rhys's cryptic note, *"where dead things bloom."* It was remote, isolated, and soundproof the perfect place for abuse, or perhaps, for a victim to be permanently contained.

A surge of fear ran through him. He was being maneuvered. Anya wasn't just isolating Rhys; she was isolating both of them. She was tightening her control, moving the perceived threat out of the main house.

"The conservatory is quite cold, Mrs. Ashworth," Cillian said, pushing back gently. "Rhys is sensitive to the damp."

"He will wear a coat," she replied, her voice leaving no room for argument. "The move is final. I require complete silence in the main house while Alistair is away."

Cillian yielded, realizing that further resistance would only lead to his immediate dismissal.

The conservatory proved deeply unsettling. It was vast, dusty, and cold, filled with the skeletal remains of tropical plants pressed against tall, grimy panes of glass. It felt less like a room and more like a beautiful, broken cage.

Cillian looked at Rhys, sitting quietly at the small antique table they had brought in. The boy appeared pale and fragile against the looming glass walls.

"We'll be okay here," Cillian whispered, trying to sound confident.

Rhys just nodded, his wide eyes fixed on Cillian. He didn't seem afraid of the room itself only of the woman who had forced them into it.

Cillian knew then that he couldn't wait for the senator's return. Anya was setting the stage for something final. The rescue had to happen now, before she used this soundproof glass cage for something irreversible.

CHAPTER 13
RHYS'S DRAWING

The forced tutoring sessions in the cold, isolated conservatory only heightened Cillian's sense of urgency. Anya had provided them with a disturbing amount of privacy, confirming Cillian's fear that she was planning something.

He knew the time for tutoring was over. He was now operating purely as a rescuer.

During a break, while they were reviewing historical maps, Cillian leaned in close.

"Rhys. Listen to me. The Senator is gone. Your mother is tightening her control. We have to go. Soon."

Rhys went rigid, his pupils dilating slightly. "Go where?"

"Away. Out of here. Somewhere safe. I have proof of everything the notes, the control. We can get to London, find help."

Rhys was silent for a long moment, his thin fingers gripping the edge of the antique table.

"She'll find us," he said quietly. "She always knows."

"She won't," Cillian promised, his voice firm. "We'll leave before dawn. We'll use the service door and my car. Can you be ready?"

Rhys didn't answer right away. Instead, he reached for a blank piece of parchment and a charcoal pencil Cillian had brought for art history. He began to sketch quickly, his hand moving with a strange, frantic precision. He didn't look up until he was finished.

He slid the paper across the table and said abruptly, "I need to use the washroom. I'll be right back."

Before Cillian could react, Rhys disappeared through the service door.

Cillian picked up the sketch. It was rough but unmistakable: a stick figure trapped inside a large, simple cage with thick black bars. Outside the bars stood a towering figure Anya her face featureless but radiating menace. Beside the cage stood a smaller, clearly drawn figure of Cillian, positioned exactly where he needed to be to open the lock.

The drawing broke him. It wasn't just a quiet "yes." It was a desperate cry for help a visual plea that captured everything Rhys couldn't say out loud. This was what Cillian was risking his career and freedom for. Rhys was relying on him completely.

Cillian folded the drawing carefully and tucked it into his jacket pocket, his eyes stinging. The evidence was overwhelming, both physical and emotional.

He heard Rhys's light footsteps returning through the service door. Cillian met his gaze.

"Tomorrow morning," he said, his voice thick with resolve. "I'll be ready."

Rhys nodded, a flicker of something unreadable relief, maybe even determination crossing his face. The moral weight of his decision was immense, but Cillian felt a strange, deep calm. He was no longer just Cillian the tutor. He was Cillian the rescuer.

He would get Rhys out of the glass cage before Anya Ashworth could shatter them both.

Chapter 14
The Final Plan

The plan was stark, simple, and terrifyingly close. Cillian waited until after dinner, when Anya had retreated to her main-floor office and the house manager, Mr. Finch, was busy locking up the downstairs wings. He found Rhys waiting near the entrance to the servants' staircase a prearranged meeting spot near the kitchen.

They didn't speak in full sentences; they whispered fragments of logistics, their words snatched and swallowed by the echoing silence of the hall.

"My car keys," Cillian confirmed, tapping his jacket pocket. "Hidden here. I'll get the small bag I packed for you."

Rhys nodded, his eyes wide and luminous in the dim light. "I'll wear the dark coat. My boots are ready."

"We'll use the service door," Cillian reiterated, tracing the route in the air. "It leads out to the small courtyard where my car is parked. We'll be on the road in ninety seconds. No noise. No lights until we hit the highway."

"The evidence?" Rhys whispered, tilting his head toward Cillian's chest.

Cillian patted the breast pocket containing his phone and the small, heavy journal tucked inside the trinket box. "It comes with us. Proof of everything. We'll show the police the journal first, once we're safe in London. Anya won't be able to talk her way out of those words."

Rhys gave a slow nod, but his expression was shadowed.

"There's something else."

Cillian leaned closer, apprehension tightening his throat. "What is it?"

"I can't sleep," Rhys confessed, his voice trembling slightly. "It's the stress the fear of tomorrow. I'm afraid she'll know. I'm afraid I'll panic and make a sound." He looked vulnerable, utterly dependent on Cillian. "Could you bring me a glass of water tonight? Just before you go to bed? It helps me calm down."

Cillian felt a surge of tenderness. Even in this high-stakes conspiracy, Rhys was still just a terrified boy. "Of course, Rhys. I will. You'll be fine. Just be ready."

Rhys looked up, his gratitude profound. "Thank you, Cillian. You're the only one."

Cillian quickly retreated to his room. He removed his car keys from his jacket pocket and placed them on the bedside table. Then he checked his backpack a small, dark athletic bag he would use to carry essentials and the evidence. He placed the trinket box and the car keys inside.

He glanced at the clock: 11:30 p.m. Seven hours until their escape. He felt a deep, unshakable sense of righteousness. He was breaking the cycle of abuse and saving a life.

Cillian set the alarm on his watch for 6:30 a.m., ensuring it was a silent, vibration-only alert. The weight of the car keys and the evidence box felt heavy and real. He was ready. He was committed.

There was no turning back now.

Chapter 15
The Alibi

Cillian couldn't sleep. The mix of cold dread and wired adrenaline made lying down impossible. The house was silent now, wrapped in the deep, heavy darkness of the countryside. It was 1:15 a.m.

He kept his promise to Rhys, creeping down to the kitchen. He filled a glass with filtered water, the sound of the running tap deafening in the stillness. Then he climbed the servants' stairs up to Rhys's wing. The boy's door was slightly ajar another sign of trust.

Rhys was sitting up in bed, looking small and pale. "Thank you, Cillian," he whispered, accepting the glass with both hands. "You don't know what this means."

Cillian murmured a reassurance, and as he spoke, Rhys quickly brought the glass to his lips. Cillian's eyes drifted for a moment to a framed family photo on the bedside table a rare picture of Rhys and his father, Alistair, smiling awkwardly. When he looked back, Rhys had finished the water.

Cillian returned to his room, but the unease persisted. His phone lay beside his backpack his vault of evidence. He felt exposed. If they were caught, the Ashworths' power would crush his story instantly.

He needed a lifeline. He needed someone to know why he was doing this.

Unlocking his phone, he opened his email and found Daniel's address his former colleague. Cillian began to type a frantic, raw message, letting his paranoia and righteous anger spill out.

Subject: *UNSTABLE SITUATION – URGENT*

Daniel,

I know you think I'm overreacting, but you have to listen. I'm living in an unstable environment. The mother, Anya, is not just cold she is mentally unstable and dangerous. I have proof photos of her journal, where she details her methods of psychological containment and control over Rhys. She has been systematically isolating him and threatening him. I saw the marks.

I'm terrified she's planning to have him institutionalized, or worse. The atmosphere here is suffocating. I have reason to believe I'm being watched, and my termination is imminent. I can't call the police; her husband is Alistair Ashworth, and they would cover it up.

I am getting Rhys out of here before dawn. I have documentation. If anything happens to me, or if I go silent, or if you hear a story about me being "unstable" or "obsessive," you need to know that it's a lie. I am saving a child from a monster.

This is my last message. Please, if you see this, know the truth.

Cillian

Cillian reread the email. It sounded unhinged. It sounded desperate. It sounded exactly like the confession of a man losing his grip on reality. But it was the truth. It was a paper trail an alibi declaring his true motive.

He hesitated for a full minute, his finger hovering over *Send.* The danger of sending it was immense, but the danger of silence was Rhys's life.

He tapped *Send.*

The email vanished into the digital void a beacon of truth and a marker for his inevitable destruction. Cillian placed the phone in his backpack and felt a deep, exhausting calm settle over him. He had done all he could.

He lay down in the dark, staring at the ceiling. Just three hours until 6:30 a.m. He closed his eyes, convinced he had just secured their freedom unaware that Rhys had watched the light under his door until the very second that damning email was composed and sent.

Cillian had not built an alibi; he had completed the frame.

PART II

THE INVESTIGATION

Chapter 16
The Silent Watch

Cillian jerked awake thirty minutes before his alarm. It wasn't the silence that woke him; it was the sound of something shifting something nearby.

He held his breath and listened. The house was usually a tomb at this hour, but tonight there was a subtle, almost imperceptible presence.

He slipped out of bed, adrenaline flooding his system. Moving quietly, he crept to his door and pressed his ear to the wood. He heard nothing but the pounding of his own heart. Yet the feeling persisted: he was being watched.

His gaze fell on the backpack on the floor, the heavy presence of the evidence vault inside. He needed to stay alert.

He tiptoed to the window and peered into the darkness. The grounds were invisible beneath a thick blanket of pre-dawn mist. The air was cold and damp.

Then he saw it.

Near the service door, right next to where his car was parked, there was a faint, almost invisible light the kind of pale glow that only appeared in the darkest hour of the night. It seemed to come from inside, maybe a utility room or a window left partially uncovered. But it shouldn't have been on. The staff wouldn't be stirring for hours.

Cillian felt the muscles in his jaw tighten. Anya. She was awake. She was watching.

He checked his watch: 6:00 a.m. Too early for the escape.

He dressed quickly in dark clothes and pulled on a thick sweater. Slinging the backpack over his shoulder, he checked his phone one last time. The email was sent. The password was secure.

He had planned to wait for the vibration alarm, but the sight of that faint, distant light told him everything. Anya was circling. She knew something was wrong, and she was preparing to strike.

Cillian opened his door a sliver. The hall was pitch black. He listened again. The only sound was the heavy, oppressive quiet of the Ashworth Estate. The silence wasn't protective it was expectant.

It was waiting for him to make the first move.

He knew he couldn't wait until 6:30 a.m. He had to go now. Rhys would be waiting. He had to be.

Cillian crept out of his room, the backpack a lead weight on his back. He moved silently down the servants' staircase, his heart hammering out a panicked rhythm that threatened to betray him.

The investigation was officially underway and the first lesson was clear: he was the one being hunted.

Chapter 17
The Past Tense

The aborted escape left Cillian stranded in his room, the adrenaline hangover leaving him shaky and defeated. He had crept back upstairs after seeing the light, convinced that Anya was waiting by the service entrance. He hadn't dared approach Rhys's room, terrified of leading Anya straight to the boy.

The rest of the night passed in a cold, anxious vigil. Cillian sat awake, staring at the clock, waiting for the safety of morning light. He knew his rash move earlier had likely confirmed the Ashworths' suspicions.

The next morning, his breakfast was brought up to the attic by the house manager, Mr. Finch, who delivered the tray without meeting Cillian's eyes. It was a clear, calculated act of isolation. Cillian was now officially locked out of the main house and cut off from observation.

Trapped in his attic room, Cillian felt the walls closing in. He had to use this isolation to his advantage. He needed more context. Pulling out his evidence phone, he connected it to his limited personal data plan.

He typed two words into the search bar: **Ashworth Estate tutor.**

The first few results were polished links to Senator Ashworth's campaign site, emphasizing the family's dedication to privacy and their philanthropic work. Cillian filtered the search to local news archives, digging back five, six, seven years.

The data loaded slowly maddeningly slowly. Then, a headline from a small regional online paper flickered onto the screen:

25-Year-Old Ashworth Family Tutor Quietly Terminated After "Instability"

Cillian's fingers trembled as he tapped the link. The article was short, dated five years ago around the time Rhys would have been eleven.

The story identified the former tutor as a young man named **Tobias Hale.** It stated that Hale had been "escorted off the property" after displaying "erratic and aggressive behavior." The Ashworths' PR firm had issued a statement expressing regret that Hale's "personal instabilities interfered with his professional duties." The article mentioned that local police were briefly involved but quickly cleared the Ashworths of any wrongdoing.

The phrase *personal instabilities* hit Cillian hard. It was the same language the senator had used in his email about Cillian's "overwhelming empathy" being a "flaw."

This was it. This was the "last one" Rhys had cryptically mentioned. Tobias Hale had seen the same pattern of abuse, tried to intervene, and had been expertly framed, silenced, and dismissed as a madman.

Cillian reread the article, searching for any detail that might expose the lie. He found a quote attributed to "a source close to the family," claiming that Hale had become "obsessed with Mrs. Ashworth" and had begun exhibiting "paranoia."

The comparison was terrifyingly clear. Tobias Hale's story was Cillian's future. The narrative was already written the unstable, empathetic tutor who fixated on the mother and eventually lost his grip.

Then came the chilling realization: Tobias Hale hadn't been driven away by Anya; he had been framed by Rhys, using the same psychological playbook. Cillian understood now that he was merely repeating the role, making the same mistakes, reinforcing the same official story that would destroy him.

Cold terror settled in his chest. He wasn't the first to try to break the cage. He was just the next pawn.

He glanced at his backpack, the evidence box secured inside. His final communication with Daniel suddenly looked less like an alibi and more like a prewritten confession of madness signed by his own hand.

Cillian knew he was in a race now, not against Anya's temper, but against Rhys's calculated, five-year-old plan. He had to assume Rhys knew everything about the previous tutor and had refined his method specifically for him.

The realization that he wasn't special just predictable was the most terrifying truth of all.

CHAPTER 18
RHYS'S WARNING

The isolation ended abruptly that afternoon when Cillian was summoned back to the conservatory for a tutoring session. Anya was absent a small mercy Cillian barely registered.

Rhys was waiting, his face a portrait of manufactured distress.

"Cillian," he whispered immediately, glancing nervously toward the service door. "I heard them this morning. They were talking about the security light near the service entrance. Mom was angry."

Cillian's blood ran cold. The light he had seen. Rhys had either overheard the conversation or was skillfully capitalizing on Cillian's growing fear.

"Did they mention me?" Cillian asked, keeping his voice low.

Rhys shook his head quickly. "No, but she was talking about Tobias the man before you."

Rhys had never spoken the former tutor's name aloud before. Cillian stared at him, the fear inside him escalating. Rhys was confirming the information Cillian had found, proving he was still on Cillian's side.

"She said that Tobias became… unstable," Rhys continued, his voice trembling slightly, perfectly echoing the language Cillian had read in the news report. "She said he started searching the house, looking for things that weren't there. She said he lost his job because he grew obsessed with proving she was hurting me."

Rhys leaned closer, his eyes wide and pleading. "She made it sound like Tobias was crazy, Cillian. But I know he wasn't. He just scared her and she had the power to make everyone believe him."

This was Rhys's most skillful manipulation yet. By repeating the false narrative and reframing it as Anya's cover-up, he completely validated Cillian's paranoia. Cillian felt a surge of loyalty, convinced Rhys was risking everything to warn him.

"She can't do that to you, Rhys. Or to me," Cillian said firmly. "I have the journal. She can't deny those words."

Rhys shuddered dramatically. "She has endless places to hide things. She keeps everything near the house manager's office all the records, all the keys to the locked rooms. If Tobias was looking for physical proof, he wouldn't have found it in the library. He would have checked Mr. Finch's records."

Rhys paused, letting the clue sink in. "And Cillian, be careful with the phone. They watch the digital devices. Tobias was obsessed with his phone. If they find it, they won't just prove you're unstable they'll erase everything you found."

The warning was precise, directed, and completely wrong. Rhys wasn't protecting the phone; he was ensuring Cillian kept it full of digital evidence, knowing exactly where it was hidden. He was pointing Cillian toward the next fatal step: the physical search of Mr. Finch's restricted area.

Cillian thanked Rhys, his resolve hardening. He had to find physical proof that Anya was drugging or isolating Rhys, confirming the intent written in the journal, before Rhys's safety or Cillian's freedom was irrevocably lost. He needed access to the house manager's private records.

CHAPTER 19
THE PRESCRIPTION

Rhys's warning about Mr. Finch's records pushed Cillian into action. Anya was still absent, likely busy spinning her story to the Senator over the phone about Cillian's supposed "instability."

Mr. Finch's private office was next to the kitchen wing, far from Cillian's attic room, making it risky to access. Cillian spent an entire day observing the house manager's routine. Finch was meticulous with his schedule, but he always took his lunch break between 12:30 and 1:30 p.m., usually driving into town.

The next day, Cillian waited. At 12:35 p.m., he heard the faint crunch of Finch's car tires on the gravel outside. He quickly slipped down to the main floor. Finch's office door was locked, but on the same antique key ring he'd used for the journal was a smaller, modern-looking key. Retrieving the ring from its hiding spot, he tried the key. It clicked open instantly.

The office was plain and smelled faintly of paper and disinfectant. Ignoring the filing cabinets, Cillian focused on a small, locked medical supply cabinet near the desk. From his bag, he pulled out a delicate lock-picking tool something he'd bought weeks ago after learning from a YouTube tutorial. As he worked, he felt the familiar mix of shame and adrenaline.

It clicked open.

Inside, among the bandages and antiseptics, were several prescription bottles. Cillian photographed each label with his evidence phone.

Anya Ashworth's bottle was for Lorazepam, a powerful anti-anxiety and sedative medication prescribed in a high dosage. Cillian immediately suspected that Anya was either using it to cope with her own cruelty or as a means to keep Rhys compliant.

Senator Alistair Ashworth's bottle was for a restricted sleeping aid, one requiring special approval. To Cillian, it confirmed the Senator's willful ignorance. He was medicating himself into oblivion to avoid facing his wife's abuse.

The final bottle bore Rhys Ashworth's name. It had been prescribed by a child psychiatrist known for treating severe behavioral issues. The medication was an atypical antipsychotic.

Cillian felt sick. Antipsychotics? Anya wasn't just isolating Rhys she was drugging him into obedience, slowly breaking down his mind to preserve her perfect image. The journal entries "contain him," "obedience" now felt like they directly described these pills.

He returned the bottles, closed the cabinet, and locked the office door behind him. The antique key ring went back to its hiding place. Then he retreated to his room, his supposed victory hollow and heavy.

He now had undeniable proof of Anya's chemical control over her son. The realization burned in him like fire. This wasn't just an escape anymore it was an extraction from a pharmaceutical prison.

CHAPTER 20
THE EMPTY CHAMBER

The next piece of the puzzle Cillian needed to address was the remote shed Rhys had cryptically led him past the one Cillian instinctively felt held physical secrets, perhaps a hidden room or the tools of torture.

Cillian waited until dusk, finding a moment when Mr. Finch was occupied supervising the evening maintenance routine. He took the large, gothic iron key from the antique key ring and found, with a heavy clunk, that it unlocked the door to the remote workshop.

He slipped inside.

The shed was disappointing. It was meticulously clean and orderly, smelling strongly of wood stain and old motor oil.

There was no dungeon, no secret room only neat shelves containing specialized tools, gardening equipment, and spare parts for the heating system.

Cillian swept his phone's flashlight beam around, desperately searching for a hidden catch or a loose floorboard. Nothing.

He was defeated. Anya had been too careful.

Then he noticed a small, secured box on a workbench labeled *First Aid and Hobbies.* He forced it open. Inside, he found standard bandages and gauze but also a bottle of liquid latex and a small palette of theatrical makeup used for creating fake wounds and scars.

Cillian stared at the materials. Liquid latex. He immediately recalled the purple-and-yellow bruise he had seen, how real it had looked and how perfectly rendered.

He quickly dismissed the thought. Rhys wouldn't do that to himself, he told himself firmly. This must be for the Senator's political stage perhaps to make him appear injured during a public service event. Or maybe it was Rhys's own sad attempt to hide real injuries with makeup. The latter seemed more plausible a desperate victim using fantasy to cope.

Cillian photographed the first aid kit as proof that the house contained specialized supplies, evidence that Anya might have used tools to cover up injuries. He closed the box and replaced it exactly as he had found it.

He left the shed, locking the heavy iron door behind him. The shed had been a dead end, but the lack of physical evidence only strengthened his belief that the Ashworths relied on sophisticated psychological and chemical abuse not crude physical violence. He would have to keep searching for the ultimate proof of their wicked intent.

CHAPTER 21
THE SECRET COMPARTMENT

Anya remained absent, but Cillian knew he couldn't wait any longer. He needed something irrefutable something that connected the psychological control (the journal) and the chemical control (the pills) to a permanent plan. He needed evidence of institutionalization.

Cillian focused on Senator Alistair Ashworth's private office, the center of the family's power. He remembered the Senator's desk calendar from his earlier research a simple, often overlooked item.

The office door was unlocked. Cillian stepped inside and began searching the desk. Among the drawers, he found an old, seemingly forgotten desk calendar from three years ago. On the anniversary of the Senator's political appointment, a handwritten sequence of six numbers caught his eye.

He tried the sequence on the electronic safe hidden behind the bookcase. A quiet, triumphant beep followed. The safe door hissed open.

Inside, Cillian found financial ledgers, land deeds, and, stacked beneath them, a folder labeled **"Rhys – Legal."** His heart pounded as he pulled it out. The top document was a recent, heavily notarized amendment to Alistair Ashworth's will.

Cillian scanned the dense legal text, searching for key phrases. His eyes froze on a chilling line in a contingency clause:

"...in the event that Rhys is deemed a danger to himself or others, I hereby grant the estate power to commit him to a secure, specialized facility in the Cayman Islands, managed by the appointed foundation, ensuring zero media access and absolute lifetime care."

Cillian felt the blood drain from his face. This wasn't just manipulation it was the final stage of their plan. Anya wasn't simply controlling Rhys; she and the Senator were plotting to permanently exile him, imprisoning him in a remote facility under the guise of "care."

The note in the journal *must contain him for the stability of the family* wasn't symbolic. It was literal.

Cillian photographed every page of the will amendment with his evidence phone. This was it. Irrefutable. His final piece of proof.

He carefully replaced the documents, closed the safe, and stood still for a moment, dizzy from the weight of what he had uncovered.

He wasn't saving Rhys from an abusive mother he was saving him from a life sentence of isolation, planned by his powerful and corrupt parents. The escape was no longer urgent. It was absolutely essential.

CHAPTER 22
THE EMOTIONAL TOLL

The discovery of the will pushed Cillian past his breaking point. He was no longer just an investigator; he was a terrified man, responsible for saving a life against impossible odds.

The combination of isolation, fear, and sleep deprivation began to wear him down. He hadn't slept properly in days. He couldn't shake the image of Rhys wasting away in a facility in the Cayman Islands forgotten and medicated into oblivion.

He spent the morning pacing his attic room, the floorboards groaning under his weight. Again and again, he pulled out the evidence phone, staring at the blurred photos of the journal and the will, as if needing physical proof that his mind hadn't invented the entire conspiracy.

He kept glancing out the window. The grounds were vast, but they offered no escape only constant, oppressive green. Every shadow felt like a lurking observer. He imagined Anya hiding behind the enormous oak trees, binoculars trained on his single attic window.

Suddenly, a loud, sharp caw echoed from the roof a crow landing heavily on the slate tiles above him. Cillian jumped. The sound hit him like a shock, and he stumbled backward into his desk. His heart pounded against his ribs. He was convinced the noise was a signal, a warning, or a sign that Anya was finally coming for him.

He rushed to the window, eyes wide with wild, unchecked paranoia. But he saw nothing only the silent, stretching grounds below. His mind twisted the image of the crow into something mechanical, a drone sent by Anya to watch him.

In a burst of blind panic, Cillian slammed the window shut with violent force, the wooden frame rattling in protest. He yanked the heavy velvet curtains closed, plunging the room into darkness, and collapsed against the wall, gasping for air.

He had to get out. He was losing his grip.

Unbeknownst to him, Anya Ashworth was walking the perimeter path far below, speaking quietly on the phone to her PR agent about Alistair's upcoming conference. She glanced up at the sudden, forceful movement in Cillian's window the sharp slam, the drawn curtains.

Anya paused her conversation. The movement was abrupt, aggressive, and deeply unusual. She frowned, a cold, calculating expression settling over her face.

He's spiraling, she thought, confirming the senator's earlier suspicion that Cillian was unstable. *It's happening faster than we expected.*

She resumed her call, her tone cool and controlled, but she mentally filed away what she had just witnessed as vital information.

Cillian, still breathing hard in the dark attic room, looked into the small mirror on his wardrobe. He didn't see Cillian, the empathetic tutor. He saw a frantic, exhausted man with dark circles under his eyes, his hair wild, his clothes disheveled.

He saw Tobias Hale.

The truth was, Rhys didn't need to do anything to prove Cillian's instability. Cillian was doing that all on his own.

CHAPTER 23
THE DISTANT CALL

The incident at the window terrified Cillian. He needed validation one single voice outside the Ashworth matrix to confirm that he was not losing his mind. He needed his friend, Daniel.

He waited until late afternoon, when Rhys was supposedly having his mandatory rest period and Anya was still in her office. He retrieved his phone and dialed Daniel's number, a frantic urgency making his hands shake.

Daniel answered, his voice bright and busy, clearly preoccupied with London life. "Cillian? Hey, man, I got your email. Don't worry, I looked into it"

"Daniel, listen to me," Cillian interrupted, his voice a low, urgent rasp. "The email? It wasn't paranoia. It's worse. I found his father's will. They're going to put Rhys away permanently. A secured facility, overseas. And the mother she's drugging him. I found the pills, Daniel. Antipsychotics."

Cillian paused, waiting for the necessary shock, the validation.

But Daniel's voice flattened. "Cillian, hold on. Wait a second. You sound completely stressed. Seriously, you need to take a few days off."

"No! I'm not stressed! This is proof! I have pictures of the will and her journal entries! It confirms everything!"

"Okay, look," Daniel said, his voice now careful, patronizing. "I read your email. You mentioned a 'cold, unstable wife' and 'psychological containment.' Now you're talking about stolen pills and a secret will. This is exactly what I mean. You're spiraling, mate. You need to come home."

"They're going to destroy him! And they'll destroy me, just like they destroyed the last tutor! Tobias Hale, Daniel! Look him up! It's the same story!"

"I don't know who that is, Cillian. You're talking about conspiracy theories. Look, you need professional help. I'm worried about you."

Cillian felt a surge of desperate rage, betrayed by the one person he trusted. "You're useless! You're exactly what they want you to be a complacent idiot who believes the powerful family's narrative! I'm doing this alone, then. Just know the truth when they spin the story."

He slammed his thumb down on the End Call button. He hadn't convinced Daniel; he had only confirmed his friend's worst fears about his mental state. The call hadn't been a lifeline it had been the final, definitive step in severing his ties to reality.

He was truly alone now, trapped within the house, fueled by anger and righteousness, and officially branded "unstable" by his last external contact. The escape was now a secret war, and Cillian was officially losing the perception battle.

CHAPTER 24
RHYS'S EMPATHY TEST

The failed call to Daniel left Cillian exhausted and dangerously resolved. He was alone, but he believed he was right. His only ally was Rhys.

That evening, during their tutoring session in the cold conservatory, Rhys was unusually quiet. He watched Cillian with deep, soulful eyes. Cillian sat tense, barely able to focus on the historical maps they were supposed to be studying.

"You look tired, Cillian," Rhys whispered at last, touching Cillian's hand lightly. The rare physical contact felt to Cillian like profound trust.

"I am," Cillian admitted, his voice raw. "I know too much, Rhys. I know what they're planning with the will. I know about the medication."

Rhys lowered his head, his voice full of carefully measured despair. "They want to lock me up forever. Just like they did to Tobias Hale."

"They won't," Cillian promised fiercely. "We're going to escape. We have the proof."

Rhys looked up, his expression shifting into one of terrible, silent judgment. "A person who would drug their own son, who would write about containment in a journal, who would ruin another innocent man's life..." He let the thought hang in the air, his eyes challenging Cillian. "Do you think a person like that deserves to get away with it, Cillian? Do you think she deserves to pay for what she's done to us?"

Cillian's righteous anger boiled over, fed by the memory of the bruise, the terrifying will, and the dismissal by his only friend. He was certain Anya was a monster who had ruined Tobias Hale and would ruin Rhys.

"Yes," Cillian hissed, the word dark and final. "She deserves to be exposed. She deserves to pay for every single thing she's done. She needs to be taken down."

Rhys nodded slowly. A deep, unsettling satisfaction flickered in his blue eyes, then was quickly masked by a look of sorrowful agreement. "I know you'll make it right, Cillian."

Unbeknownst to Cillian, Rhys held the trinket box, his hand resting discreetly on the small clasp. He was not recording their conversation, but the words were imprinted perfectly in his chillingly meticulous memory. Cillian had just given Rhys the motive, a clear, verbal confession of aggressive intent toward Anya, that Rhys needed to complete the frame.

CHAPTER 25

THE POINT OF NO RETURN

The escape was now set for the next morning. There would be no more delays, no more planning. Cillian was convinced that any further hesitation would give Anya the chance to spring her institutionalization trap.

They met briefly that evening, exchanging final whispers in the shadows of the servants' stairwell.

"The lights are out by the car," Rhys confirmed, his voice low and steady. "I checked the breakers when the house manager was distracted. It's the perfect blackout."

"Good," Cillian breathed. "I have the bag ready. The keys are in the backpack. Six-thirty sharp. I'll come to your door and tap twice."

Rhys looked down, his façade of vulnerability returning with chilling perfection. "Cillian, I'm scared. I won't sleep. The stress is too much."

He was referring to their earlier conversation, but this time there was a clear request. "I know you took photos of my mother's pills the ones that help with anxiety. If I could just have one, I could sleep tonight, and I won't make a mistake when we leave. Please. Just one. I can't risk being too agitated."

Cillian felt a moment of cold hesitation. Giving Rhys a powerful sedative crossed a professional line he had never intended to breach. But Rhys's fragile fear, combined with Cillian's conviction that the boy was already being medicated into a stupor, overrode his caution. He told himself he was saving Rhys's life a single pill to calm him was necessary.

"Where is your mother's medicine?" Cillian asked, resigned.

"She keeps them in the small locked box in her bedside table, on the first floor," Rhys whispered. "It's a simple key. On the antique ring."

The antique key ring Cillian had found. It was a final, terrible test of trust and Cillian, blinded by his protective impulse, passed it.

"I'll get it for you," Cillian promised.

He waited until 2:00 a.m., when the house was deep in slumber. He slipped the silver key off the antique ring and crept downstairs. He found Anya's room, used the key, and retrieved the Lorazepam bottle. Carefully, he shook out a single pill and placed it into a small, clean envelope. He returned the bottle and the key to their hiding places exactly as he'd found them.

Then he crept to Rhys's room and, finding the door ajar, slipped the envelope silently onto the bedside table. Rhys was curled up, feigning deep, fragile sleep.

Cillian returned to his attic room. He placed the car keys back in the backpack, next to the evidence vault. He had broken every rule, violated every professional boundary, and now unknowingly held the very tool the sedative that would be used to frame him for attempted murder.

Cillian lay down, waiting for the silent vibration alarm. He was ready to be the hero.

He had just completed the final, irreversible step into the trap.

CHAPTER 26
THE INTERCEPTION

The vibration of Cillian's watch at 6:30 a.m. was a violent shock in the stillness. He was instantly on his feet, his exhaustion replaced by pure, cutting adrenaline. He grabbed his backpack and slung it over his shoulder, the heavy weight of the evidence vault a familiar, comforting presence.

He crept down the servants' staircase for the final time. The house was utterly silent, wrapped in the cold, pre-dawn darkness. The confidence from his final preparations the lights cut near the service door, the parents deeply asleep filled him with a grim sense of control.

He reached Rhys's room and tapped twice, a soft, precise rhythm. The door opened immediately, revealing Rhys dressed in dark clothing and a large coat, his face pale and etched with fear.

"I took the pill," Rhys whispered, his voice thin. "I feel calmer. Let's go."

Cillian nodded, placing a steady hand on Rhys's shoulder. Together, they moved like silent shadows toward the kitchen wing. They passed the main hall, their footsteps muffled by the deep Persian rugs. The air in the house felt heavy and stale, like the atmosphere before a storm.

The service door was just ahead. Cillian could already picture the courtyard, his red Ford Focus, and the turn of the ignition key.

Freedom was less than ninety seconds away.

He reached out, his fingers brushing the cold metal of the latch when suddenly, the vast main hall lights exploded into life.

The incandescent glare was blinding, assaulting his night-adjusted eyes. Cillian flinched violently, raising his arm to shield his face, his heart vaulting into his throat. Standing directly ahead, blocking the hallway to the service door, were Anya and Alistair Ashworth.

They were fully dressed. Anya wore a severe black dress, her posture rigid, her eyes like chips of pale ice. Senator Ashworth stood beside her, his face a mask of disappointment and fatigue. They looked less like captors and more like judges about to deliver a verdict.

Cillian froze, his mind spinning between sheer terror and burning fury. They hadn't been asleep. They had been waiting.

"It's over, Mr. Rains," Anya said, her voice cutting through the silence like a scalpel. "The game is over."

Panic seized Cillian's chest, but conviction kept him standing. They had been caught, yes but not defeated.

He yanked his phone from his backpack, his hands shaking as he unlocked it. "No, you don't!" he shouted, his voice breaking the tense stillness. "You won't institutionalize him! I know about the will! I know about the pills! I have the proof right here!"

He thrust the phone forward, ready to expose the photographic evidence of their cruelty.

Rhys stumbled back, his hands flying to his mouth, eyes wide, playing the perfect image of a terrified child caught between two warring adults.

Chapter 27
The Staged Argument

The hall had become a frozen scene of confrontation. Cillian, shouting accusations and clutching his evidence, faced the Ashworths, who remained disturbingly calm. Rhys stood between them, trembling violently.

"Institutionalize him?" Alistair repeated, his brow furrowed in what Cillian recognized as a masterful act of feigned confusion. "We were discussing seeking specialized therapeutic care, Mr. Rains as outlined in the contingency clause you clearly accessed illegally."

"Therapy? You call that therapy?" Cillian shouted, his voice raw. "Lorazepam and antipsychotics! I saw the prescriptions! I saw the journal where you wrote about *containing* him!"

Anya took a slow step forward, her expression shifting into a mask of controlled devastation. "Cillian, you have dangerously misinterpreted documents you stole. I wrote that journal while dealing with a severe anxiety crisis after Alistair's first campaign threat. It was about controlling myself, not Rhys."

That lie delivered with such cold authority only fueled Cillian's rage. "Don't lie to me! I know what you did to Tobias Hale, and you won't do it to Rhys!"

Rhys suddenly let out a high-pitched, terrifying scream. It wasn't the sound of a fragile child; it was the raw, unrestrained cry of a teenager losing control.

"STOP IT!" Rhys screamed, turning on his mother. "Why do you always do this? Why do you always have to control everything? You can't even let him leave without a performance! I hate you!"

He swung his arm wildly, slapping Anya across the arm. The motion was violent, fueled by sudden, volatile anger that was genuinely shocking.

Anya flinched backward, her composure cracking for a moment as genuine fear flashed in her eyes. It was the movement of someone who had seen that kind of rage before.

Cillian stared, stunned. This was it, Rhys fighting back, driven by the hope of freedom. The rage was real; the violence was defiance made flesh. Rhys wasn't the silent victim anymore he was the hero, breaking free from his abuser.

Cillian's heart swelled with pride and vindication. He threw his phone back into his backpack and stepped forward, wrapping a protective arm around the boy.

"See?" Cillian shouted triumphantly at Anya. "You broke him! His defiance is the proof of your cruelty! You deserve this, Anya!"

"Stay away from my son!" Anya cried, her voice thick with genuine terror. But her fear wasn't aimed at Cillian it was directed past him, at Rhys.

Alistair finally stepped in, moving to shield his wife with a protective arm. He looked utterly defeated. He didn't look like a wicked politician he looked like an exhausted father caught in an ongoing catastrophe.

But Cillian, blinded by his conviction, saw only the final act of an enabling coward protecting his monstrous wife.

CHAPTER 28

CILLIAN'S EVICTION NOTICE

The physical altercation, though brief, shattered the last remnants of civility within Ashworth Hall. Rhys stood panting, his shoulders rising and falling, the picture of a child pushed past his limits. Cillian held him tightly, the backpack strap digging into his shoulder.

Anya Ashworth, one hand pressed to her chest, struggled to steady herself. She stared at Cillian with a mix of blazing hatred and deep, exhausted sorrow.

"Alistair, look at him," she whispered to her husband, her voice trembling with panic. "He's completely lost it. The calls, the surveillance, the aggression it's Tobias Hale all over again."

Alistair sighed heavily and turned his weary, bloodshot eyes on Cillian.

"Mr. Rains," he said, his voice low and deliberate. "You've crossed a line that cannot be uncrossed. You've trespassed, stolen personal property, and physically confronted members of my family. Effective immediately, your contract is terminated for gross unprofessionalism and obsessive behavior."

Cillian scoffed. "Obsessive? I'm exposing child abuse! I have proof of your plan to institutionalize him!"

"You have distorted, stolen material," Anya cut in, her tone regaining its icy control. "And you've proven your instability in front of witnesses."

Alistair raised a hand to silence her. "I'm giving you one chance to leave quietly. You will vacate the premises at once. Mr. Finch will drive you. You must be off the property within the hour. If you're still here at noon, or if you attempt to contact Rhys in any way, I'll call the police for trespassing, theft of classified documents, and harassment. Your career will be finished, Mr. Rains."

The threat was sharp and final. Cillian felt the walls closing in. They had turned everything against him. What had begun as a desperate rescue now stood framed as the downfall of an unhinged tutor. His good intentions had been twisted into the perfect lie.

A chill of dread swept through him. He had to protect Rhys, but he couldn't fight the Senator's power. Not now. Not while the evidence was still on his phone.

He glanced at Rhys. The boy's wide, terrified eyes met his, silently begging for help. Cillian leaned close and whispered urgently, his voice low enough for only Rhys to hear.

"We're still going," he said. "Just a delay. Be ready."

Then he turned, the backpack still on his shoulder, and walked out of the hall under the cold, watchful eye of Mr. Finch. He was a fallen hero, cast out from the cage. But as Cillian stepped through the doors, one truth burned inside him he was leaving the real victim behind, trapped with the monster.

CHAPTER 29

THE FAMILY DINNER

Cillian was confined to his attic room for the rest of the morning, with Mr. Finch standing guard like a silent sentry downstairs. He couldn't risk leaving until the last possible moment he needed to protect his phone and the evidence from any potential search.

Senator Ashworth had returned, cutting short his overseas trip to deal with the crisis Cillian had caused.

At 11:00 a.m., Cillian was summoned to the dining room for what was clearly meant to be a final, forced breakfast. The atmosphere was suffocating.

Anya sat at the head of the long mahogany table, perfectly composed in a fresh cream suit. Her eyes were cold, showing no trace of the previous night's turmoil. Alistair sat at the other end, listlessly picking at his eggs. Rhys was beside his mother, small and withdrawn, staring down at his plate.

"A rather unprofessional exit, Mr. Rains," Alistair said, breaking the silence. His voice was flat, carrying only a hint of restrained reproach. "Your actions last night confirmed our earliest doubts about your suitability."

Cillian refused to respond. He ate quickly, his eyes moving between Anya and Rhys, searching for one last sign proof of the abuse.

He watched Rhys's hands, clasped tightly under the table. Then, he saw it: Anya's left foot, sliding subtly beneath the linen tablecloth, pressing lightly against Rhys's leg. It was almost imperceptible a small, deliberate warning followed by a faint tightening of her jaw.

Cillian's conviction hardened. Even here, in front of her husband and Cillian, Anya was controlling him. That gentle pressure was a threat, silencing Rhys before he could speak.

He glanced at Alistair, who still stared at his plate, avoiding all eye contact. In that avoidance, Cillian saw the truth: Alistair was a coward an enabler too afraid of his wife's quiet cruelty to protect his own son.

"I wish Rhys well," Cillian said suddenly, standing and dropping his napkin onto the table. "I hope he finds freedom someday."

The words hung in the air like a blade. Anya's eyes flared with pure venom, but Alistair didn't look up. If anything, he looked relieved.

"Your termination papers are ready, Mr. Rains," Alistair said stiffly, nodding toward Finch. "Please be expedient."

He rose and left the room at once, clearly eager to escape the tension Cillian had drawn into the open. He was abandoning his son to the monster.

Cillian knew then that his final, desperate attempt to save Rhys had to happen now. He had to leave behind one last message a beacon of truth.

CHAPTER 30

THE FINAL DECEPTION

Cillian quickly grabbed his bag and started down the servants' stairs, ready to face Mr. Finch and the main gate. Just then, a faint whisper stopped him.

"Cillian. Wait."

Rhys was standing on the landing above him, his face a mask of sorrow. He had clearly slipped away from his mother during her post-breakfast briefing with Finch.

"You can't leave without the evidence," Rhys whispered, his voice trembling. "I know you're taking the photos with you. But what if they search you at the gate? You have to hide it somewhere they won't look."

Rhys looked around frantically, his eyes landing on the remote, unused shed near the perimeter. "The workshop! They only use it for storage. Hide the phone there. Send the police an anonymous tip after you leave. Use the photos from London."

The idea was brilliant desperate, yet flawlessly logical. Hiding the phone would keep the evidence safe and protect Cillian from arrest until he could act from a secure distance. He was stunned by Rhys's quick thinking.

"You're right," Cillian breathed, pulling the evidence phone from his bag. "I'll do it. I'll call the police as soon as I get out of the county, Rhys. I promise. I'll expose her."

Rhys stepped closer, his large blue eyes glistening with tears. "I know you will. You're the only honest person here." He reached into his coat pocket and pulled out a small, crumpled piece of paper a note written on a torn corner of a newspaper.

"Just… take this," Rhys whispered, pressing the note into Cillian's hand. "It's nothing. Just a goodbye. I wrote it last night, hoping you'd read it once we were safe. Don't open it until you're on the road."

Cillian felt his heart ache. The gesture was painfully sincere a final, tangible piece of their bond. He tucked the note into his inner jacket pocket, close to his heart, where it would be safe.

"I won't forget you," Cillian promised, his voice thick with emotion.

He turned and slipped away, rushing toward the front gate. Rhys stayed on the landing, watching him go.

Cillian never saw the subtle, triumphant smirk that crossed Rhys's lips as the tutor disappeared from view. Rhys knew exactly where Cillian was going to hide the evidence. More importantly, he knew exactly where the police would find that crumpled note a final, perfect piece of the frame.

Cillian left the house believing he was carrying the truth to safety and leaving behind a helpless boy. In reality, he had just delivered the last, deadly ingredient in Rhys's master plan: a fully justified, seemingly unhinged scapegoat.

Chapter 31
The Final Drop

Mr. Finch drove Cillian's Ford Focus while Cillian sat rigidly in the passenger seat, his eyes fixed on the house shrinking in the rearview mirror. Finch was silent, his face expressionless a perfect, loyal employee.

Cillian's heart pounded in a desperate rhythm as he pulled out his phone. He had to follow Rhys's plan exactly.

"Stop the car, Mr. Finch," Cillian ordered, his voice clipped and rough.

Finch didn't argue. He pulled the car over sharply near the edge of the remote property, right across from the low iron gate leading to the workshop shed.

"I left something behind," Cillian said, forcing his tone to stay neutral. "A set of tools for Rhys. I need to make sure they're secure."

Grabbing his backpack, Cillian ignored Finch's cold, questioning stare. He unlocked the shed gate with the large iron key and slipped inside. He found the workbench, pulled out his evidence phone, and hid it deep inside the cavity of an old, rusted metal filing box. He secured it with a heavy chain, just as Rhys had instructed.

Safe.

He locked the shed door behind him and hurried back to the car.

Finch drove the rest of the way in silence. When they reached the massive gates of the Ashworth Estate, Finch stopped the car, handed Cillian the keys, and stepped back.

"Senator Ashworth asks that you do not contact this house or any member of his family again, Mr. Rains. For your own protection."

Cillian ignored him, started the engine, and sped down the road, leaving the grim fortress behind.

Miles away, on a quiet country lane, Cillian finally pulled over. He reached into his jacket pocket and unfolded the crumpled note Rhys had given him a small, torn piece of newspaper. His heart swelled with a desperate need for connection as he read the words, written in small, careful handwriting, slightly smudged by Rhys's hand:

"I hope you see the dawn of freedom. Thank you for your strength. You are my light."

Cillian slumped against the steering wheel, relief flooding through him in a dizzying wave. The sacrifice, the fear, the paranoia it was all worth it. He had a brave ally, and the evidence was safe.

He immediately tried to call Daniel, pulling up the contact on his car's interface. The call failed no service. He tried again. The signal was weak and unreliable. He swore under his breath.

He had to keep driving until he reached a major town with a reliable signal then he could call the police and tell them exactly where to find the evidence.

CHAPTER 32
THE SIREN SONG

Cillian drove for twenty minutes, his focus fixed on the road and the flickering *No Service* icon on his phone. He was heading toward the county seat, where he could use a landline or a stable signal to contact the police far away from Alistair Ashworth's influence.

For the first time in days, he felt a measure of calm. Rhys was safe, at least for a few hours. The evidence was secure. He had broken free.

Then, suddenly, a piercing, high-pitched wail cut through the quiet of the morning.

Cillian looked in his rearview mirror. Far down the road, fast approaching, were flashing blue lights. Not one car, but two, moving at high speed.

He pulled over, assuming they were heading to an accident. But as the cars sped closer, Cillian saw the distinctive black-and-white markings of the local constabulary. And they weren't turning off the highway they were heading straight toward the Ashworth Estate.

A surge of triumphant vindication rose in Cillian's chest. Rhys must have found another way. Maybe he had convinced Mr. Finch to make the call. The plan was already in motion!

Cillian pulled back onto the road, following at a cautious distance. He needed to be there when the police found the will and the journal. He needed to be the witness the one who confirmed Rhys's story.

He was about four minutes behind the police cars when they reached the Ashworth gates. The officers didn't stop; they used a remote code, and the massive gates swung open instantly. Cillian pulled up just as they were clanging shut again.

He slammed on the horn repeatedly until the house manager, Mr. Finch, appeared, looking grim and composed.

"They're investigating Anya Ashworth!" Cillian shouted through the window. "I called them! I have the proof!"

Finch's face stayed unreadable. "The police were called, Mr. Rains. But not by you. And they are here to investigate an emergency, not Mrs. Ashworth."

Finch spoke quietly into his sleeve. Moments later, one of the police cars an unmarked vehicle backed out of the gate and drove straight toward Cillian's Ford.

A tall, imposing woman in a dark suit stepped out. Detective Inspector Miller. Her expression was grave, and her eyes were fixed on Cillian.

"Mr. Rains," she said, her voice calm but carrying the full weight of authority. "We've received a highly distressing report. Please step out of the vehicle slowly. You are currently under suspicion of harassment and violation of a protection order."

Cillian felt reality shift and tilt. He hadn't called the police. Rhys had. But Rhys hadn't called them to expose Anya. Rhys had called them to frame *him.*

CHAPTER 33

THE TURNAROUND

Cillian's mind scrambled for footing. "Protection order? That's insane! She's the abuser! I'm the one with the evidence!"

DI Miller remained unmoved. "The evidence, Mr. Rains, suggests otherwise. We have a detailed, distressed report filed by Mrs. Ashworth hours ago, describing her fear following your aggressive behavior last night. Please comply."

Cillian's conviction was immense, but his legal position was nonexistent. He was the unstable ex-employee shouting accusations at the gates of a powerful Senator. He stepped out of the car, heart pounding, the backpack feeling less like evidence and more like a mark of guilt.

Desperate to regain control of the narrative, he pleaded, "I put the real evidence in the shed! The workshop on the perimeter! The photos of the will, the journal they prove she was institutionalizing Rhys!"

Miller exchanged a quick, weary glance with the officer beside her. "We will investigate your claim, Mr. Rains. But first, you are being detained for questioning."

Cillian was placed in the back of the unmarked police car. The ride up the long, sprawling drive was agonizing. He stared out the window, expecting to see Anya celebrating her victory.

Instead, when they reached the portico, the scene was one of quiet chaos. Alistair Ashworth stood on the steps, pale and shaken, speaking urgently into a phone. Mr. Finch was nearby, supervising two paramedics who were rushing medical equipment toward the house.

Cillian turned to Miller. "What's happening? What's wrong?"

"There's been a medical emergency," Miller said evenly. "A severe sedative overdose. Both Senator Ashworth and his wife, Anya."

Cillian blinked, unable to process the words. Sedative overdose? The only sedative he knew of was the Lorazepam he had retrieved and given to Rhys last night a single pill meant to calm the boy.

Panic set in. He looked around wildly. Where was Rhys?

Miller escorted Cillian into a side room, guarded by an officer. Cillian shouted, "Rhys! Where is Rhys? He's the victim! He's the only witness!"

Moments later, Rhys entered, accompanied by a police constable. The boy was weeping uncontrollably, clinging to the officer's arm. His face was a perfect picture of trauma broken, terrified, and innocent.

Cillian watched in horrifying slow motion as Rhys's eyes met his. The boy's expression twisted into one of pure, unfiltered fear and disgust.

"Stay away from him!" Rhys cried, voice shaking with terror as he pointed straight at Cillian. "He tried to hurt them! He tried to hurt my parents!"

The truth hit Cillian like a physical blow. The final, deadly stroke of the sociopath's brush. Rhys had never taken the pill Cillian gave him. He had used it to poison his parents.

And now Cillian the empathetic tutor who tried to save him was trapped in the ultimate lie.

Chapter 34

The Perfect Victim

The small side room instantly became an interrogation chamber. Rhys was removed quickly, leaving Cillian alone with Detective Inspector Miller.

"I didn't do it, Inspector," Cillian insisted, his voice trembling but firm. "I gave him one pill one sedative last night, at his request, to calm him. I didn't drug his parents. Rhys did this."

Miller sat down slowly, pulling a thick folder onto the table. "Rhys Ashworth is a traumatized sixteen-year-old, Mr. Rains. His testimony is perfectly consistent. Yours is, frankly, spiraling into conspiracy."

He opened the folder, revealing a printed copy of Cillian's desperate email to Daniel. "This email, sent from your device at 1:15 a.m., explicitly details your fixation on Mrs. Ashworth, your claim that she is 'mentally unstable and dangerous,' and your intent to 'take her down' and 'get Rhys out.' We were notified of this email, which is why we were alerted to your potential threat to the family."

Cillian shook his head violently. "That was my belief based on her journal, the will! You have to find my phone it's in the shed! It has the photos of the will amendment the institutionalization clause!"

"We'll investigate all your claims, Mr. Rains," Miller replied evenly. "But let's look at what we *do* know. Rhys told his father that you, a dismissed employee, were obsessively searching for his mother's medication and had made threats against her life. Rhys was the one who called emergency services this morning when he found his parents unresponsive saving their lives."

Miller tapped the email with his finger. "Your own words show your intent to make her 'pay.' Now both parents are in critical condition from a massive sedative overdose. The sedative was Lorazepam the same drug prescribed to Mrs. Ashworth, which you admitted having access to and retrieving last night."

Cillian felt a cold, sinking wave of defeat. Rhys had anticipated every move he would make, weaving it perfectly into the story of Cillian's supposed instability. The police had everything they needed.

"The will," Cillian whispered, clinging to his last thread of hope. "Ask Alistair about the will. Ask him why he wanted to send Rhys to the Cayman Islands."

Miller sighed deeply, his expression heavy with disappointment. "You need to calm down, Mr. Rains. We're taking you into custody now. Anything you say can and will be used against you."

CHAPTER 35
THE MISSING KEY

Cillian refused to yield. As the officers moved to restrain him, he fought not out of aggression, but out of desperation. "The shed! You have to check the shed! The rusted metal box! The evidence vault!"

Miller halted the officers. "You're saying the evidence that proves your innocence is in the shed?"

"Yes! Rhys told me to hide it there! He said they wouldn't look! Please, Inspector, it proves everything!"

Miller looked at the constable. "Take a unit and check the remote workshop on the perimeter. Look for a phone in a metal box."

The next hour was agony. Cillian sat restrained, listening as the medical team worked frantically on the Ashworths upstairs. Every passing minute felt like a lifetime. He waited for the police to return with the phone the proof that would finally expose Rhys's perfect lie.

At last, the unit returned. The constable approached Miller, shaking his head.

"The workshop was locked, Inspector," the officer reported. "We opened it with the master key. There's only gardening equipment and old supplies inside. No metal box with a phone. Nothing unusual."

Cillian screamed, a raw, primal sound of pure betrayal. "He moved it! He moved it! He set me up!"

Miller looked at Cillian with absolute, cold certainty. "The only person setting anyone up, Mr. Rains, is you."

She then retrieved a small, crumpled object from the evidence bag. It was the note Rhys had given Cillian the one he had tucked close to his heart.

"We found this note hidden in the lining of your jacket," Miller said. "It's written in Rhys's hand. Perhaps you can explain its contents, Mr. Rains."

Miller smoothed out the paper. The tears Cillian thought were Rhys's had smudged the ink. The original words *You are my light* were now blurred and twisted, transformed into something dark and condemning.

Miller read the smudged words aloud: "I will never forgive you for what you tried to do to my family."

The note Rhys's final, perfect touch now stood as undeniable proof of Cillian's guilt, and of Rhys's role as the victim.

Part III

The Reversal

CHAPTER 36
THE INTERROGATION

The formal interrogation began hours later at the station. Cillian was facing attempted murder charges. Detective Inspector Miller sat across from him, her empathy completely extinguished and replaced by the grim focus of a prosecutor.

Cillian's story the secret will, the journal, the abuse, the rescue mission sounded increasingly absurd, a web of paranoia and circumstantial evidence spun by a desperate, disgraced employee.

Miller didn't raise her voice. She simply presented the facts.

"You violated a protection order. You admitted to administering sedatives. Your emails confirm a psychotic breakdown and aggressive intent toward Mrs. Ashworth. And your supposed evidence has vanished."

Cillian fought back, desperately revealing the real secrets, trying to find one crack in her composure.

"Tobias Hale! Look into the previous tutor! He was framed by Rhys five years ago! It's the same pattern!"

Miller leaned forward, her expression shifting slightly.

"We did look into Tobias Hale, Mr. Rains. He spent two years in a secure facility for psychiatric evaluation after a violent incident at the Ashworth estate. He was released and is now living a quiet life. During his evaluation, Hale himself stated that he suffered from severe paranoid delusions regarding Mrs. Ashworth."

The cycle was unbreakable. Hale's own history crafted by Rhys years ago was now being used to validate Cillian's conviction.

"Alistair knew!" Cillian shouted, desperation rising again. "He was medicating himself! He saw the abuse and used sleeping pills to ignore it!"

"Senator Ashworth was under intense pressure during his last campaign," Miller replied evenly. "He was taking physician-prescribed medication for severe insomnia, as documented in his medical records, which are also included in this file. You're trying to turn a complex domestic situation into a fantasy about a crime boss and her enabling husband."

Cillian fell silent. He realized his words were only tightening the noose. He was the one who looked unstable, aggressive, and guilty. The truth, in that cold room, had become his worst enemy.

CHAPTER 37
THE CONFRONTATION

Anya and Alistair Ashworth were brought into the interrogation room not as suspects, but as official victims and witnesses, guarded by officers. They looked traumatized, but alive.

Anya's arm was in a sling a believable, staged injury from Cillian's "violent attack." Alistair was pale, still recovering from the sedative overdose at the hospital, but he held himself with rigid authority.

"Look at him, Alistair," Anya whispered, her voice trembling with carefully crafted sorrow. "He's still trying to frame us."

Cillian felt a sudden surge of clarity. He had to strike with the one thing they couldn't possibly have prepared Rhys for the medical diagnosis.

"Rhys isn't the victim!" Cillian shouted, ignoring Miller's warning glance. "He's the monster! Ask them about the diagnosis! Ask them about his Antisocial Personality Disorder!"

Alistair flinched. Anya's eyes narrowed. Cillian had finally hit a nerve.

"You have no right to confidential medical information!" Alistair thundered, slipping into his Senatorial authority.

"You kept it secret because you're terrified of him!" Cillian roared back. "The will, the pills, the abuse of Tobias Hale it's all Rhys! He drugged you, Alistair! He drugged you with the pill I gave him! He wanted you both dead!"

Alistair looked at Miller, his face a mask of weary defeat. "This is exactly the paranoia we warned you about, Inspector. He's spinning a delusion to avoid responsibility."

But then, standing beside her husband, Anya looked directly at Cillian. Her icy composure cracked for the first time. She gave him a small, almost imperceptible nod. A flicker of absolute terror and sorrow crossed her face.

It was the silent, undeniable confirmation Cillian had been waiting for. Anya knew. Alistair knew. They were terrified of their own son. Cillian had been right all along only he had aimed his fight at the wrong person.

CHAPTER 38
THE REFRAMING

The nod from Anya was Cillian's absolute truth but it was also his final moment of clarity before his world collapsed. Miller, sensing the sudden shift in the room, turned to Alistair.

"Is there any information regarding Rhys's medical history that you need to disclose, Senator?"

Alistair looked at his terrified wife, then at the defeated figure of Cillian. He exhaled slowly, the sound heavy with years of suppressed anxiety.

"Yes," Alistair said at last, his voice barely above a whisper. "Rhys has complex behavioral needs. He was diagnosed with a form of Conduct Disorder years ago, which later developed into traits of Antisocial Personality Disorder. He has a history of pathological lying and manipulative behavior."

Cillian stared at him, the full weight of the revelation crashing down. Rhys wasn't the victim he was the orchestrator.

Alistair continued, his tone regaining strength as he addressed Cillian directly.

"The institutionalization clause in the will that wasn't meant to punish him, Mr. Rains. It was the only way to ensure he could be contained if his behavior became dangerous, to protect the public. The journal entries? Those were Anya's anxiety notes her attempts to manage his violent mood swings and control the information leaking about his condition."

Anya's voice was hollow when she spoke.

"The bruise you saw? He learned how to fake them from online videos. He used theatrical makeup from the shed the liquid latex the same one you dismissed as 'political props.' He wanted you to believe I was hurting him so you'd trust him... and risk yourself."

Cillian fell back into his seat, his mind spinning as everything in the house reassembled itself into a terrifying new picture:

- **The Locked Journal:** Not a cruel diary, but a desperate mother's guide to survival.
- **Tobias Hale:** Not framed by Anya, but driven insane and silenced by Rhys, who was testing his methods.
- **The Escape:** Not a rescue, but the final step in Rhys's plan to eliminate his parents and frame the unstable tutor he had carefully cultivated for weeks.

Rhys was brought into the room calm, composed, and accompanied by a social worker. He looked at Cillian with a perfectly studied expression of disappointment and fear.

He stepped closer, stopping just out of reach, and leaned in. When he spoke, his voice was low meant only for Cillian. It was no longer frightened; it was controlled, smug, and chillingly adult.

"You really thought you were the hero, Cillian?" Rhys whispered, a faint smile touching his lips. "You were just a tool. The most perfect tool I've ever built. Tobias was too easy. You were empathetic, arrogant, and determined. You were flawless."

Rhys paused, letting the horror settle like poison in the air.

"And thank you," he added softly. "The Lorazepam was exactly the final touch my coffee needed."

Rhys stepped back, his face instantly twisting into a mask of absolute, paralyzing fear. He let out a piercing, delayed shriek and stumbled backward toward his parents.

"He's still dangerous!" Rhys cried, clinging to Alistair's arm. "He's still trying to hurt us! He tried to poison you, Dad!"

Alistair wrapped an arm around his son, his face drawn with exhaustion and pain. He tried to project strength for the police, though his hands trembled slightly.

Suddenly, Alistair coughed a sharp, rattling sound. His eyes rolled back, his grip slackened, and he fell forward, collapsing heavily onto the interrogation room floor.

Anya screamed and rushed to his side. As she bent over him, her body wavered. Her eyes glazed over, and she collapsed directly on top of her husband.

Chaos erupted. Officers rushed to the fallen couple, shouting for medics.

The sedatives. The single pill Cillian had given Rhys was Lorazepam, but both Alistair and Anya were already under immense stress. Alistair had been taking strong sleeping medication, and Anya relied on anti-anxiety pills. Rhys hadn't simply given them the pill he had slipped it into their early morning coffee. The result was a fatal combination, one that reacted disastrously with Alistair's prescription drugs and Anya's medication.

Police swarmed the room, calling for paramedics. Detective Miller stared from the collapsed couple to Rhys, who now stood completely still. His eyes were wide, his lips trembled slightly, and he watched the chaos with a strange, detached curiosity.

Then, as if on cue, Rhys broke into high, keening sobs. He ran to the nearest officer. "He did it! Cillian did it! He must have put something in their coffee! He wanted them dead so I would be all his!"

The officers believed him immediately. Cillian, restrained and frozen in horror, could only watch the flawless execution of Rhys's frame. The truth was right there, yet it condemned him completely. He was guilty by association, by motive, by his own actions.

Miller turned to Cillian, her face set like stone. "The sedatives, Mr. Rains. The Lorazepam you admitted to possessing we found the empty envelope."

She glanced toward the chaos surrounding the lifeless Ashworths, then looked back at Cillian. "You're under arrest, Mr. Rains. Attempted murder. You had motive, means, and documented aggressive intent."

Chapter 40
The Aftermath

The noise was deafening ambulance sirens, police radio chatter, and the constant, heartbreaking wails of Rhys Ashworth. Cillian was dragged away, his own screams of "He did it! He framed me!" lost in the chaos.

A search team, guided by Rhys's calculated instructions, found the discarded Lorazepam container smeared with Cillian's fingerprints from his clumsy attempt to retrieve it. It was discovered exactly where Rhys claimed Cillian had tossed it in a "panic." The single pill inside now represented a massive, near-fatal overdose.

Cillian was transported to the local lockup.

His story was simple: Rhys, a sociopathic teenager, had manipulated him into becoming the perfect scapegoat.

The police case, informed by Rhys, was simpler still: Cillian, an unstable and obsessive employee fixated on Rhys's mother, had attempted to abduct the child and murder the parents in a jealous, psychotic rage.

The evidence was damning the frantic email (Exhibit A), the violent confrontation, the stolen medication, the empty shed (proving Cillian had lied about the phone), and finally, the tearful testimony of the heroic son.

The news broke the following day and became an instant sensation. Senator Ashworth was in critical condition; Anya was in a coma. The tragic hero was Rhys the brave son who had alerted emergency services and was now being praised for his courage in the face of a violent psychopath.

Cillian sat in his cold cell, staring at the grey walls. He had failed. He hadn't saved Rhys; he had simply become the most effective tool Rhys had ever used.

He clung to one last, desperate thought a fragment of hope: the final message he had sent to his friend Daniel. He prayed, with quiet, hollow terror, that Daniel would finally find a signal, receive the text, and somehow look inside the shed the same empty shed Cillian had checked and uncover the truth.

But deep down, Cillian knew the devastating reality: Rhys was smarter, faster, and more ruthless than he could have ever imagined. The sociopath hadn't just created a crime he had created a martyr.

Cillian was the monster.

And Rhys was the perfect son.

CHAPTER 41

THE USELESS DEFENSE

Three weeks bled into four. Cillian was held without bail, the public fervor surrounding the attempted murder of Senator and Mrs. Ashworth making his release impossible. The media, fueled by sanitized press releases from Alistair's chief of staff, had crucified Cillian portraying him as a deranged opportunist seeking vengeance after being justly fired.

Cillian's court-appointed solicitor, a perpetually stressed woman named Helena, sat across from him in the sterile meeting room, her face etched with profound weariness. She was entirely unconvinced of his innocence.

"We need to discuss your plea, Cillian," Helena said, rifling through the thick file, which seemed to consist mostly of

Cillian's own frantic emails and Miller's official report. "The prosecution is considering a reduction from attempted murder to conspiracy to harm and severe assault, given that the Lorazepam dosage wasn't immediately lethal. If we push this to trial, we'll lose. Your emotional instability, documented in your own email to Daniel, is too strong a defense for the prosecution."

"My emotional instability is manufactured by Rhys," Cillian argued, leaning forward, his voice low and intense. "He is a clinical sociopath. He set up Tobias Hale five years ago, and he perfected the performance on me. Helena, he drugged his own parents! He orchestrated the entire thing to eliminate his father's control and put his mother in a coma!"

Helena sighed, pushing her glasses up her nose. "Cillian, I've read the psychiatric reports on Rhys. They indicate profound trauma from a chaotic home life, resulting in severe emotional regulation issues. They do not indicate a homicidal mastermind. The fact remains, you confessed to retrieving the medication. Your fingerprints are on the container. Your email provides a clear motive: you wanted to see the mother pay."

Cillian slammed his fist quietly on the table. "The phone! He made me hide the phone in the shed! It had photos of Anya's journal and the will! It proves my motive was sound!"

"The police searched the shed, Cillian. It was empty. You have to stop clinging to this phantom evidence. It makes you look delusional. I can argue manslaughter due to psychosis, but I can't argue innocence based on a missing phone and a fifteen-year-old boy you insist is a professional criminal."

Cillian suddenly recalled a detail. "Rhys asked for the sedative at 2:00 a.m. I hid the phone in the shed at noon the next day, after I was dismissed. Rhys was still in the house. He had ten hours to get the keys to the shed, empty the box, and put the keys back."

Helena stared at him blankly. "You're asking me to prove that a teenager broke into a locked shed on his own property, anticipated your exact hiding place, emptied the contents, and returned the keys all while recovering from a supposed kidnapping attempt? Cillian, the narrative is that you planted the evidence yourself, then invented a story about Rhys stealing it when it didn't materialize."

Cillian slumped back, the truth a suffocating weight. Rhys had calculated every move, including Cillian's final, desperate attempt to secure the evidence. The shed wasn't a hiding place it was a final, empty test that Cillian had failed.

CHAPTER 42

THE MEDIA DARLING

The public disgrace intensified, fueled by Alistair Ashworth's carefully managed PR machine. Cillian became the face of unchecked arrogance and psychopathic obsession.

The focus shifted entirely to Rhys the brave survivor. Local news ran continuous coverage: *"The Hero Son: Rhys Ashworth Saves Parents from Psychotic Tutor."*

Rhys appeared on camera, flanked by a social worker and his father's chief of staff. Alistair remained hospitalized, in critical but stable condition. Anya was still in a deep coma, the sedative damage proving more catastrophic than anyone had first believed. The doctors' reports were vague but confirmed severe neurological trauma.

Rhys delivered a short, tearful statement, looking directly into the camera. He wore the same coat he had on during the failed escape.

"It was terrifying," Rhys whispered, his voice cracking with perfect, cultivated sorrow. "Mr. Rains... he became obsessed with my mother. He told me he hated her and wanted her gone. He saw me as his only chance to control the family. I was afraid, but I knew I had to tell my father. I thank God I was fast enough to get help before he succeeded."

His performance was devastatingly effective raw, honest, and completely believable. He cried just the right amount, his eyes showing deep, lasting trauma rather than calculation.

Cillian, watching the recording of the press conference in the sterile silence of the lockup, felt physically sick. Rhys was using Cillian's own words the confession that Anya deserved to pay as proof of his malice.

The narrative was airtight. Rhys had displayed trauma, loyalty, and courage. Anya, silent in her hospital bed, was the helpless martyr. Alistair, clinging to life, was the wounded statesman.

And Cillian was the convicted monster.

The only detail Cillian clung to was Anya. She was in a coma, but not dead. She was the only person who had looked at him with understanding. She was the only remaining witness to Rhys's true nature and she was silent.

CHAPTER 43
THE LOST EVIDENCE

Helena, Cillian's solicitor, returned with a face grimmer than usual.

The prosecution has filed a motion to introduce the recovered email and Rhys's original handwritten note as the core evidence of premeditated conspiracy," she stated, sliding a copy of the motion across the table. "They argue the note is irrefutable proof of Rhys's panic and your aggressive intent."

Cillian ignored the legal jargon. He was focused only on the logistics of his defeat.

"Helena, did they ever check the filing box in the shed again?" he asked.

"No. Why would they? It was empty."

"Because Rhys lied about it being empty," Cillian hissed. "He told me to hide the phone there when Finch dropped me off. Finch then drove away, and I sped off in the opposite direction."

Cillian grabbed a napkin and drew a quick diagram. "Rhys was still inside the house, dealing with his parents' 'overdose.' The police sirens had only just arrived. He had only a few minutes before they reached the workshop."

He paused, a chilling realization spreading through him. "But Rhys didn't need to go all the way back to the workshop to get the phone. He needed the shed key back, which was still in my car the car I drove away in. He couldn't have accessed it."

Helena frowned. "Then the phone was never there, Cillian. You're delusional."

Cillian shook his head slowly, the cold truth settling over him. "No. I drove away, yes. But I stopped on the country lane to read Rhys's note and try to call Daniel. That note he gave me... it was a delaying tactic."

"The moment I drove out of sight, Rhys knew I would stop, thinking I was free," Cillian whispered, his eyes widening in horror. "He had his keys and his composure. He simply slipped out the service door during the chaos of the ambulance's arrival, ran to the shed with his own key, retrieved the phone, and returned to the house while the police were focused on the overdose victims. The metal box was empty only because he had been there minutes before the police arrived."

The logic was flawless, terrifying, and utterly impossible to prove. Rhys had calculated Cillian's exact delay the emotional need to read the note and contact Daniel and used that small window of relief to complete the framing. The note wasn't a confession; it was a trap perfectly timed.

Helena glanced at the napkin diagram, then back at Cillian. "I appreciate the narrative, Cillian," she said quietly. "But the prosecution has Rhys's tearful testimony and your email. We need to prepare for sentencing."

Chapter 44
The Family Meeting

Senator Alistair Ashworth woke up in the intensive care unit. He was pale, weak, and haunted. The doctor confirmed that his recovery would be long, but Alistair would survive.

His sister, Martha, was waiting patiently by his bedside. Martha was a quiet, silver-haired woman his only immediate living relative besides Rhys.

"Alistair," Martha whispered, holding his frail hand. "You look terrible. But thank God you're awake."

"Rhys. How is Rhys?"

"Rhys is coping, dear boy. He's a martyr now. The entire country knows his name. He's been staying with me, as Anya… well, Anya hasn't woken up."

Alistair closed his eyes, tears slipping out from beneath his lids. "Anya. He broke her, Martha. He finally broke her."

"Cillian broke her, Alistair," Martha corrected gently. "That obsessed tutor who nearly killed you both."

Alistair opened his eyes and stared at the ceiling. "No. Cillian was… a catalyst. Yes, the final act. But Rhys… Rhys has been like this since he was a child. The lies, the rage, the calculated isolation. The diagnosis. We hid it. We thought we could control it with the antipsychotics."

He turned his head, his voice raspy. "We were terrified of him, Martha. We knew he needed that facility the institutionalization clause Cillian found was the only thing that gave us leverage. But he knew we wouldn't use it. We were cowards."

Martha rubbed his arm soothingly. "You were good parents, Alistair. You were dealing with a troubled boy who eventually snapped when a predatory adult Cillian fueled his instability."

Alistair sighed, accepting the easy lie the palatable truth. It was simpler than admitting his son was a murderer. "Rhys needs stability, Martha. He needs a quiet place, away from the estate, away from the media. He needs someone calm, someone kind. I can't be that person right now, and Anya might never be again."

Martha looked at her nephew's picture the innocent, grieving face of the heroic son plastered across the hospital room television. "I understand. I'm lonely, Alistair. I have plenty of room. I'll take care of Rhys."

Alistair nodded, relief washing over him. He was safe. Rhys was contained. The Ashworth name was protected.

He had given his monstrous son to the kindest, most unsuspecting person he knew.

Chapter 45
The Move

Rhys moved to Martha's suburban home a week later, accompanied by a social worker. The contrast with the Ashworth Estate was immediate and jarring. Martha's house was smaller, warmer, and filled with the gentle clutter of a life lived for others knitting needles, comfortable chairs, and the smell of home-baked bread.

Martha, Alistair's sister, was retired, kind, and deeply empathetic. She was exactly the sort of person who read articles about trauma survivors and believed wholeheartedly in the power of unconditional love.

Rhys played his role flawlessly. He was quiet, polite, and deeply mournful. He spoke sparingly, mentioning his trauma only in vague, heartbreaking terms.

"I just want the chaos to stop, Aunt Martha," Rhys whispered one evening, his head resting lightly on her shoulder as they watched a news report about his father's slow recovery. "I just want to be normal."

"You are safe here, dear boy," Martha assured him, holding him close. "The monster is gone. He can't touch you now."

Rhys nodded into her shoulder, but his eyes were open, surveying the room. He noted the placement of her medication simple blood pressure pills and vitamins the location of her small safe tucked beneath a loose floorboard near the fireplace (revealed when Martha bent down awkwardly to retrieve kindling), and the schedule of the cleaning woman, who arrived every Thursday at 9:00 a.m. sharp.

Martha's vulnerability was structural, not just emotional. She was kind but slow, slightly forgetful, and utterly trusting.

Rhys was patient. He knew the Ashworth money was currently locked in a foundation controlled by his father's legal team, contingent on Alistair's full recovery and Anya's guardianship status. He couldn't touch the real wealth yet.

But Martha's personal finances her modest pension, her savings, and the deeds to her warm, comfortable home were ripe for the taking. He needed new resources to establish his permanent freedom.

Rhys settled into the guest room, placing his few belongings neatly in the dresser. He unpacked the trinket box and, for the first time in weeks, pulled out the phone he had recovered from the shed and the Lorazepam bottle now empty, perfectly cleaned, and ready for disposal. He checked the phone. The photos of the will and the journal were still there: perfect, pristine proof of the real truth, waiting to be destroyed at the right moment.

The game had begun again, only this time, the stakes were Martha's peace and sanity not Cillian's.

CHAPTER 46
THE FINAL ATTEMPT

Cillian's trial date was set for four months later. He was drowning in hopelessness. Helena insisted he plead diminished responsibility due to trauma bonding.

In one last desperate act, Cillian invoked his right to a brief, monitored, and recorded phone call to an outside party. He called Daniel.

The call was static-laced and tense. Daniel answered reluctantly, clearly fearing Cillian's renewed madness.

"I know what you're doing, Cillian," Daniel said immediately. "Don't try to manipulate me. I've seen the news."

"I know you have," Cillian replied slowly, ignoring Helena's frantic hand gestures to stick to the script. "I'm not asking you to believe me, Daniel. I know you won't. I'm asking you to check one thing."

"What?"

"The shed," Cillian whispered. "The workshop on the edge of the Ashworth property. It's locked with an iron key. Rhys planted the Liquid Latex there. It's theatrical makeup for bruises. He used it on himself. It's proof that Rhys is the one manufacturing the physical evidence."

"Cillian, the police said the shed was empty"

"They lied! Or Rhys emptied the metal box, but he would never have thought to clean the supplies. The Liquid Latex is proof he stages the injuries. If you find the bottle, Daniel, you prove the bruise was a lie. And you prove Rhys is the master of deception."

Cillian knew this was a long shot. Rhys was meticulous, but that little shed held the supplies for the first lie Cillian ever saw. It was a detail Rhys might have overlooked in his focus on the grander evidence.

"Find the theatrical makeup, Daniel," Cillian repeated, his voice firm. "If you find it, you find the real Cillian. If you don't... then I'm exactly who they say I am."

The line went dead. Daniel, sweating and agitated, looked down at his clean desk. He ran a hand through his hair, shook his head, and immediately deleted Cillian's number, cutting off their final connection.

The thought of checking the shed was too much too close to Cillian's terrifying madness. He was safe in London. And so, he let Cillian's final, desperate plea vanish into the air.

Chapter 47
The Verdict

The trial was a spectacle quick and brutal. The prosecution presented a mountain of circumstantial evidence, all forged by Cillian's own actions and framed perfectly through Rhys's trauma.

The star witness was Rhys Ashworth sixteen, frail, tearful, and impeccably articulate. He recounted Cillian's descent into a "terrifying obsession," his threats against Rhys's mother, and his final, desperate act of violence. Rhys described finding his parents collapsed, his quick thinking to call 999, and his sorrowful discovery of Cillian's twisted note. His performance was flawless, instantly winning the sympathy of both jury and judge.

Alistair Ashworth, thin and leaning on a cane, testified to Cillian's "aggressive lack of professional boundaries."

Helena, Cillian's lawyer, delivered a half-hearted defense based on "diminished capacity" and emotional overload, fully aware she could not overcome the formidable power of Rhys's testimony.

Cillian's claim that Rhys was a sociopath never reached the jury. It was too explosive too easy for the prosecution to dismiss as a desperate conspiracy theory.

The jury deliberated for only five hours.

The foreman rose, his expression grim. Cillian stood motionless, the sterile courtroom fading around him.

"On the charge of conspiracy to cause grievous bodily harm, how do you find?"

"Guilty."

"On the charge of aggravated assault," the framing of the altercation "how do you find?"

"Guilty."

Cillian felt a cold, final sense of relief. It was over. He had been defeated publicly and legally by the most perfect villain he had ever encountered.

Chapter 48
The Price of Empathy

Sentencing was passed two weeks later. Cillian received ten years for conspiracy and assault, deemed a risk to society because of his documented instability and obsessive fixation.

He was transferred to a maximum-security facility. He was no longer Cillian the tutor he was Inmate 4099, the man who had tried to murder a senator and his wife.

He received one final piece of correspondence: a news clipping forwarded by the prison chaplain. It detailed the state of the Ashworth family. Alistair was recovering and had resumed his duties, though he appeared visibly frail. Anya remained in a permanent vegetative state, requiring constant care in a private medical facility. Her trauma was complete.

Cillian stared at the words, realizing the ultimate cost of his empathy. Rhys had achieved exactly what he wanted his father weakened by illness and trauma, and his mother permanently silenced.

Cillian folded the clipping, his movements slow and deliberate. He had once believed his empathy was a strength; now he saw it as a deadly, predictable weakness. Rhys had simply pulled at the thread of Cillian's protective instinct until the entire fabric unraveled into violence and paranoia.

He looked at the iron bars of his cell. Rhys had used the heavy gates of the estate to symbolize a cage now Cillian was in a real one. The final, chilling irony was that the only person who knew he was innocent Anya was trapped in an even deeper, unyielding prison: her own mind.

CHAPTER 49
RHYS'S NEW NARRATIVE

Nine months passed. Rhys was thriving in the quiet, supportive environment of Aunt Martha's home. He had cemented his status as the tragic hero. He now attended a prestigious private school, excelling academically and displaying the gentle, thoughtful demeanor of a survivor. He volunteered at a local animal shelter, further strengthening his image of empathy.

Martha, meanwhile, was completely devoted to him. Her life now revolved around Rhys's needs, her loneliness banished by the presence of her "brave, fragile nephew."

One quiet Sunday afternoon, Rhys sat on the sofa reading a manuscript. It was his memoir, dictated to a ghostwriter hired by Alistair's PR team, titled *My Mother's Keeper: A Son's Story of Survival.*

Martha was sitting nearby, knitting. She paused, frowning slightly.

"Rhys, dear, I'm worried about my memory. I keep forgetting where I put my keys, and I missed my appointment with Dr. Davies last week. I'm afraid I'm becoming a burden."

Rhys looked up, his face filled with immediate, deep concern. He took her hand gently.

"Never a burden, Aunt Martha. You've given me everything. We'll find a way to manage this. I'll help you organize your medication. And about the keys... why don't we put them in that little ceramic bowl on the mantelpiece? Right where you can see them safe and secure."

Martha smiled, her anxiety easing.

"That's a wonderful idea, Rhys. You're so clever."

Rhys returned to his reading, but his eyes were calculating. He knew Martha was developing early-stage dementia. He had already discovered her small, private safe tucked beneath the loose floorboard. Inside, he had found the papers detailing her final will and testament: she had left everything to a distant niece she hadn't seen in twenty years.

Rhys knew he had to act before Martha's condition progressed to the point where her cognitive decline might complicate legal proceedings. He needed to become the primary beneficiary the devoted caregiver who deserved the inheritance.

He closed the memoir. He had perfected the narrative of the Hero Son. Now, he needed to perfect the Final Will.

He stood up, walking toward the mantelpiece, his hand brushing the ceramic bowl where Martha's keys now lay exposed.

CHAPTER 50
THE KIND STRANGER

Rhys waited until the calculated midpoint of the evening precisely when Martha's routine offered the least resistance. It was Wednesday, a quiet night with the soft glow of the television flickering across the living room. Martha, trusting and bound by habit, had just taken her evening blood pressure medication.

Rhys approached her with the gentle care of a devoted nurse, holding a warm cup of herbal tea the comforting ritual he had established weeks before.

"Aunt Martha, you look sleepy," he said softly, leaning down to place a feather-light kiss on her forehead. The physical affection felt foreign to him, but he performed it with flawless, practiced sincerity. "Why don't you get some rest? I'll finish sorting through those old legal documents Alistair asked me to organize. I know they stress you."

Martha, feeling the warmth of the chamomile and the subtle sedative Rhys had added to it, nodded faintly, her eyes already growing heavy. "That's lovely of you, Rhys. You're such a kind boy. A comfort."

Rhys stood back, watching the predictable effect of the drug take hold. She was harmless, predictable utterly compliant. Her mind, already slowed by early-stage confusion, offered no defense.

He allowed himself the first private smile of the evening a cold, thin expression that vanished as quickly as it appeared. Moving to the hearth, he knelt quietly. The small safe beneath the loose floorboard, hidden behind the kindling box, was hardly a challenge. Using the silver-tipped miniature key he had taken from Martha's key ring hours earlier, he opened the lock with a soft, efficient click.

Inside was the heavy, official will dated decades ago, along with the deed to the suburban house. He removed them carefully before pulling out his own creation: a stack of papers that had occupied his meticulous attention for the past two weeks. It was a perfectly drafted document a handwritten amendment naming Rhys as the sole beneficiary, citing his "devoted, sole care during her final years of increasing confusion."

He had practiced Martha's signature for days on spare letterhead; the looping script was now identical a perfect forgery born of patience and trust.

Rhys glanced toward the kitchen counter, where his small trinket box sat empty. He didn't need the phone or the journal anymore; the digital trail had been destroyed weeks ago, reduced to ash and vapor in a municipal incinerator. The trap was empty. The evidence against him gone.

He was meticulous, professional, thorough. All that remained was to frame the narrative: devotion and confusion, not deceit. He didn't need to frame a person this time just a story. A story of good intent.

Returning to the couch, Rhys picked up Martha's simple phone and scrolled through her contacts until he found the name of her distant niece the current beneficiary. He quickly composed a short text message, imitating Martha's vague, slightly repetitive tone.

To: Niece

Subject: My Keys

I keep forgetting where my keys are. I keep putting them in the little ceramic bowl on the mantelpiece. Please don't tell anyone. It's our secret.

He sent the text instantly. It wasn't a warning it was a timestamped piece of evidence. It served as a final, clear instruction about the safety of her possessions, cementing the narrative of Martha's growing forgetfulness just before the legal documents were irrevocably altered.

Rhys smiled as he placed the phone back on the side table. Then he inserted the new, signed will into the safe, removed the outdated one, and locked the floorboard carefully, running his hand over the carpet to ensure the threads lay flat.

He looked at Martha, sleeping peacefully, her kind, tired face resting against the cushion. He was secure. The money was his. And no one would ever suspect the hero son.

He walked to the mantelpiece and picked up the ceramic bowl the one meant for the keys turning the cold, simple object over in his hands. A wave of icy, calculated triumph ran through him. Then he reached into the drawer beneath the mantelpiece and pulled out a small, new item: a tiny antique key blank a silent, glittering memento he had taken from the Ashworth estate before his grand departure.

Rhys toyed with the cold metal, running his thumb over the uncut grooves. It was a potential door, a potential beginning. He was already calculating what this tiny, elegant artifact might unlock next. What new vault? What new life?

He looked around the warm, unsuspecting living room, then down at his own hands the hands that had administered the poison and signed the death warrant of his own freedom.

He had destroyed the arrogant tutor, Cillian, silencing the only person who had seen his truth. He had neutralized his powerful parents Alistair barely clinging to life, and Anya permanently silenced in a coma. Now, he was about to inherit his fortune from the kindest, most trusting person he knew.

Rhys slipped the key blank back into his pocket, securing the cold metal close to his hip. Then he sat down, waiting for the safety of the morning light.

The game with Cillian was definitively over. But a sociopath's life is just a series of games, and Rhys realized, with a deep, unsettling satisfaction that bordered on philosophical revelation, that the world was indeed full of kind strangers just waiting to be saved. He was their savior and they, his resources.

A NOTE FROM
THE AUTHOR

I have always been fascinated by the concept of **empathy as a vulnerability**. In the psychological thriller genre, we often assume the protagonist's conviction—their belief in abuse or conspiracy—is the absolute truth.

With **_Tutor in the Shadows_**, I wanted to turn that convention on its head. Cillian's greatest flaw isn't weakness or fear; it's his **righteous certainty**. He is so convinced he is the hero destined to save the fragile boy that he ignores every sign—the theatrical makeup, the perfect timing, the lack of physical resistance—that Rhys is, in fact, the mastermind.

The true horror of the Ashworth Estate is that the abuse was real, but the abuser wasn't the mother. It was the son, turning his parents' desperate attempt to manage his condition into the perfect, unassailable frame.

I hope you felt Cillian's agonizing descent into paranoia and, ultimately, his defeat. The greatest villains are not those who wear black, but those who wear the perfect mask of innocence.

Asher W. Lockwell

SNEAK PEEK:
THE GLASS HEIR
MARTHA'S KINDNESS TRAP

Prologue: Anya

The smell was the first thing to return. Not the cold, sterile scent of antiseptic that clung to the hospital, but the faint, cloying sweetness of jasmine and the thick, dry rot that permeated the Ashworth Estate. I was floating in a dark, silent space a prisoner of my own mind and suddenly, I was there. Back in the house.

I tried to scream, but the noise was only a faint electrical impulse in my brain. My eyes were useless, but the silence was gone, replaced by the low, constant drone of a machine that helped me breathe, accompanied by the frantic, echoing pulse of my own blood.

Anya. I knew I was Anya.

I felt pressure in my hand. Someone was holding it warm and firm. Alistair? No. The grip was too precise, too careful.

"She's recovering, Senator," a gentle, professional voice murmured in the room. "The coma is stable, but we can't be sure of the neurological impact."

Alistair's voice was hoarse, weary. "I need to know if she said anything. Before... before he was arrested. Did she say anything about Rhys?"

A nurse answered, "Only that she seemed highly agitated, Senator. She was afraid of Cillian the tutor. She kept asking for Mr. Finch and the security camera footage."

No. Not Cillian. Not the tutor. He was wrong, yes, but he was pointing the gun at the wrong monster.

I tried to squeeze the hand, to signal the truth I had seen in my final moments the look of pure, clinical triumph on Rhys's face. The truth I had confirmed to Cillian with a single, terrified nod.

The hand holding mine squeezed back a slow, deliberate pressure that sent a spike of fresh, icy terror through my paralyzed body.

"I'm here, Mother," a soft voice whispered, chillingly close to my ear. "Don't worry. The monster is gone. I'm taking care of everything now. I'm managing the affairs."

The voice was pure, perfect sorrow. A devoted son.

My mind screamed. *It's him. He's here.*

I felt a sudden, familiar shift in the air a drop in temperature. It was the scent of expensive disinfectant, old wood polish, and something sharp and metallic, like a knife.

He released my hand. A chair scraped back.

"She's resting now," Rhys's voice said, sounding weary and profoundly traumatized. "I'll be back tomorrow."

I heard the door click shut, and the silence returned deep, absolute, and full of the terrifying knowledge that the sociopath was free. And I, the only witness to his true nature, was permanently trapped, silenced, and completely dependent on the very monster who had put me there.

About The Author

Asher W. Lockwell is an author who specializes in high-stakes contemporary psychological thrillers. His work explores the intersection of moral certainty and psychological manipulation, often focusing on how the wealthy and powerful use truth and reputation as weapons.

Lockwell currently splits his time between a quiet corner of Kensington—where many of the novel's themes, such as isolation and the hidden secrets of high society, were first conceived—and the United States, where he develops many of his other novels. *Tutor in the Shadows* is his first standalone novel, cementing his reputation as a master of the domestic nightmare.

About The Publisher

MK Storyworks is a truly global book publisher, dedicated to the timeless mission of connecting compelling authors with enthusiastic readers across the world.

We pride ourselves on curating a diverse and dynamic list that spans the full spectrum of literary interests. Whether you are looking for an immersive escape into a bestselling fiction novel, seeking wisdom and knowledge from groundbreaking non-fiction titles, perfecting a dish with our acclaimed cookbooks, or introducing the magic of reading to the next generation with our enchanting children's books, MK Storyworks delivers stories that inform, entertain, and inspire.

Our commitment to quality, creativity, and global reach

ensures that every book we publish finds its place in the hands and hearts of readers, no matter where they are.

Connect with MK Storyworks

Stay up-to-date with our latest releases, author news, and behind-the-scenes glimpses by connecting with us online:

Website: www.mkstoryworks.com

Social Media:

- YouTube: @mkstoryworks
- Instagram: @mkstoryworks
- Facebook: @mkstoryworks
- X: @mkstoryworks
- Pinterest: @mkstoryworks
- TikTok: @mkstoryworks